MiKaGuRa ScHooL SuiTe
STRIDE AFTER SCHOOL

MIKAGURA SCHOOL SUITE

STRIDE AFTER SCHOOL

SADAMATSU
MINATOGAWA
• Flower Arranging Club

HIMI YASAKA
• Calligraphy Club

BIMII
? ? ?

ERUNA
ICHINOMIYA
New Student

SHIGURE
NINOMIYA
Manga Research Club

SEISA MIKAGURA
Going Home Club

KYOMA KUZURYU
Art Club

ASUHI IMIZU
Astronomy Club

YUTO AKAMA
Drama Club

STARRING SCHOOL LIFE

MiKaGuRa ScHooL SuiTe
STRIDE AFTER SCHOOL

Last Note. illustration: **Akina**

ONE PEACE BOOKS

Table of Contents

Prologue

I was thrilled to start over at a new school. It was supposed to be fun.

There would be new, cute senpai, and I could make all new friends. I could reinvent myself!

I was so excited about all the new things in store for me that I wasn't able to get much sleep. I'd set the bar as high as it would go, so I probably should have backed off and given all this a bit more consideration.

But! But! But! But!

"It wasn't supposed to be like this!"

Certainly I could be forgiven for shouting like that, my voice a little higher, and a little shriller, than usual.

But no matter how times I looked at the scene unfolding before my eyes, it showed no sign of changing.

I'd looked at it at least ten times by now. I kept shaking my head from side to side, trying to make it change. I must have looked like an insane person.

But it really wasn't a big deal.

What was unfolding before me was a striking

demonstration of one of the more *unique* aspects of my new school: Mikagura Academy. The senpai that ran the after school clubs, of which they insisted only culture-themed clubs were allowed, were throwing a welcome party for the new students

. . . But . . .

"This party is nothing, NOTHING like what I expected. Not at all! Off by 180 degrees! Everything is wroooooooong!"

Movement One: Youth Prelude

What comes to mind when you hear that there's going to be a party to welcome the incoming students?

Maybe all the clubs will put on gorgeous performances and you'll pick the one you want to join? Maybe it will be the one with that nice-looking senpai who looks like she was made to wear that uniform of hers. But then again, you wouldn't want to overlook that *other* club either, the one with the cute girl running around.

You'd probably imagine something along those lines, right? The kind where everything is full of imagination and fun and anticipation for the future? Isn't it a rite of passage that the whole country should rally to protect? Isn't it one of the most special events in a young person's life?

Maybe I was the only one who thought so highly of the parties, but at least I was self-aware enough to stop myself from going on and on about them. Still, I couldn't help but find the scene I was faced with hard to accept.

Here's an example. If you heard the Calligraphy Club would be performing something, what would you think they'd do?

You'd probably expect to see some solemn young black-haired women performing standing choreographed dance motions in silence.

"So what is with that girl? She's attacking someone with a giant brush!"

Is that the direction modern calligraphy is evolving in? Maybe I'd just never heard of it, and I was witnessing the latest, state-of-the-art techniques? No! That couldn't be right!

To make things more confusing, the Art Club was in the middle of a performance too, and it looked like utter chaos.

I expected some cute, shy girl with pigtails to stand there and softly explain the different pieces they'd made and the techniques they'd used. I was wrong! Foolish and wrong!

I wasn't going to forget the suspicions I'd given my old classmates. Thinking that I played for the *other team*, some of them had kept their distance from me. Still, who deserves to be treated like this?

15

"Why is paint flying from that palette in the air? It looks like a special attack from a fighting game!"

And besides, who would want to make an enemy of the Art Club? Wasn't it always the most gentle and peaceful club at school?

I kept rubbing my eyes to make sure I was seeing straight, but it seems that I was.

Actually, I rubbed my eyes too hard. They turned really red, so everyone probably thought that I was moved to tears by the performance.

Well to be honest, a part of me really did feel like crying. And I don't mean tears of joy.

"Ah . . ." I sighed.

It must have looked like I was sighing from satisfaction, or taking real pleasure in it all, because a guy next to me nodded passionately, as if to say that he knew how I felt.

"Don't you have anything to say?" I smiled over to the boy standing next to me. He was my senpai at the school, my cousin, and a bespectacled idiot.

"Uh . . . Welcome to the school?"

"What's so good about it!? Nothing, that's what! The only thing that's good about this is in your own head, Shigure! Ugh! You tricked me!"

"Eruna-chan! How many times do I have to ask you to call me nii-chan? Or—ah, I get it. You're embarrassed to be seen talking with me that way in public!"

"I never called you that! Not even at home! You idiot!"

I raised my arm to punch him, but he smiled as if getting punched by me was the answer to his prayers. Joy spread over his face, which disgusted me to the point where I didn't want to hit him anymore, and I shrugged it off.

"Why did I have to choose my cousin's school?"

Shigure heard my whispered complaint, and he flashed a big smile. "It's LOVE, isn't it?"

I managed to pummel him with punches before he finished talking. I threw my weight behind them, too.

My sensitive little-girl heart was screaming, "You don't weigh very much. So putting your weight into the punches doesn't help you as much as you think it does!"

The welcome party had no end in sight.

It was so loud and chaotic I could hardly believe it.

I'd certainly never seen anything like it, but everyone seemed to be enjoying themselves.

It felt like the start to a fantastic story.

*

The clock hands spin backward.

My name is Eruna Ichinomiya. I was quietly rushing to prepare for my entrance exam, though I hadn't even figured out which school I wanted to apply to yet.

I found myself saying things like, "Why do I need to take entrance exams? I think I'm just going to lay back and watch NikoNiko Douga* for the rest of my life. I'm sure I can make a job out of it somehow."

My mother was clearly on the verge of exploding at me, so I had to keep my protests to a minimum.

I was only kidding, but she freaked out and shouted at me. She cried—she despaired of the lack of trust between us.

Sure, after Golden Week* in May, I did sort of extend my vacation so I could stay in bed all day with a portable game console in one hand.

She didn't like it, but I fought back. "But MY Golden

Week is still going! Because it's MY week. Isn't it a week where you can do what you want?"

"I don't know what you are talking about. What do you mean you can do what you want? As if you do anything at all!?"

She was being stern. So I puffed up my cheeks and noisily pushed the air out with a fingertip. That would show her how much I cared.

"How can you be so relaxed? You have no reason to be so relaxed!"

"Heh, heh."

"I didn't mean that as a compliment!"

"It's MY week where I grow and thrive off compliments!"

"There you go again, lying. You don't thrive off compliments. And I'm not complimenting you!"

That's basically how our conversations always went, which explains that lack of trust I mentioned. It's like when you go to the beach, try to build a sand castle, and then give up three seconds later.

"Anyway, all I'm asking is that you get yourself into a school. I won't ask for anything more than that, okay?"

She implored, nearly begged me, to make an effort, which made me feel a little conflicted. I flipped through the stack of pamphlets from different schools that she had collected for me.

"They all look the same to me. None of them stand out in any way. Why don't they try to pique my interest by covering the pamphlets in cute girls? Of course they don't! They all just look the same. Each one is lost in a sea of sameness!"

I sat there whining about whatever came into my head when my cousin, who had permission to leave his school's dorms to come hang out, jumped in with commentary.

"Eruna-chan, you have more fun in life than anyone else I know!"

Shigure Ninomiya was two grades higher than I was and pretty good-looking. As for his grades . . . He wore glasses, which made him look like he was really smart, but his grades didn't back that up.

We'd been close since we were little, but I never wanted to pay him much attention.

My friends said things like, "*Erunantess*, your cousin is so handsome! Isn't he hot? Introduce us!"

When they got too persistent I liked to say, "Nah, he likes BOYS, especially young ones! He secretly carries around boy's love manga." I was lying, but it shut them up. I'd never actually told that friend this, but I really didn't like it when they called me "Erunantess." Did they think I was some kind of soap opera character?

What horrible sin had I committed to deserve such punishment?

Had I really done anything so bad? I don't think so!

"Hey that reminds me, Eruna-chan. The other day one of your friends told me they had a nice present for me. Then they gave me a gay romance novel. Any idea what that was about?"

Whoops. I guess I had taken it a little too far. God, forgive me! I won't do it again. Well, maybe I won't.

I repented my sins privately while Shigure, misunderstood and pathetic, looked down at the mountain of school pamphlets.

"Anyway, did you figure out where you want to apply?" he asked, concern evident in his voice. I was more worried about his reputation.

"Nope. I have no idea. I just can't make up my mind."

"Why not go to the place in your neighborhood. Your grades should be more than good enough."

"No way! Never! No way I'm going to a place like that!"

"Why not? They just renovated the building and it's supposed to be really nice."

"Their uniforms are not cute at all! I can't go anywhere with ugly uniforms!"

"So it's not that you don't want to. It's that you CAN'T. Got it. Hm . . ." he said as he looked at me, confused.

"If I have to wear an ugly uniform, I'd rather drop out!"

"If you're going to say something that pathetic, at least get that smug look off your face."

Honestly though, I really wasn't joking. The uniform design was a significant factor of my motivation for picking a school.

Girls in cute uniforms are like angels!

Or wait, were they *fallen* angels sent to tempt me? Or demons? Either way . . .

I had almost slipped into a daydream when Shigure interjected, "What about this place?"

He was holding out a pamphlet for a private school called Mikagura Academy.

Shigure went there, and that was all I needed to

know. I made a point of never opening— never even *looking*—at the thing. I couldn't even consider it.

I told him so flatly that he immediately looked crestfallen and hurt. He was always making those sad eyes at me. So I learned to ignore them a long time ago. I flipped through the pamphlet though.

"Huh. They only permit culture-themed after school clubs? I've never heard of that."

"It might be the only school of its kind. Just so you know, I'm the president of the Manga Research Club."

". . ."

"Are you ignoring me!? How dare you! Just a little— it only has to be a little tiny bit—could you please try and show some interest in what I, your beloved nii-chan, has to say? It would make me so happy!"

He was starting to ask for the impossible. It was probably the most impossible request of the century!

I tried to tell him that I thought so, but he showed me those sad eyes again. He softly shut his eyes and whimpered like a newborn puppy.

Figuring I had probably gone too far, I decided to apologize. But then I noticed that underneath his pathetic whimpering, his cheeks were flushed and a little smile tugged up at the corner of his lips, as if he was kind of happy about it all. Gross—any thoughts I'd had of apologizing vanished immediately.

I purposefully ignored him and went on flipping through the pamphlet.

And then, when I got to the school uniform page, a shockwave swept through me.

"Boom!"

"Did you just say that out loud?"

I was so floored by the pictures that I didn't even hear his stupid comment.

The first thing I noticed was the unique, and very cute, uniform design.

"How can it be . . . so . . . CUTE? It's like the kind of uniform you'd see in an erotic game!"

"You mean that in a good way?"

Wasn't that much obvious? It was the highest compliment I could come up with.

I could see it now: the school halls bustling with girls in these uniforms. Sometimes they'd get wet in the rain. Sometimes the wind would gust and pull their skirts up . . . My imagination was getting ahead of me.

And that's not all. The school had dorms, and all the students lived there.

It was too much to handle.

"Eruna-chan? What is it? Are you okay?"

"No."

"Oh, um . . . okay?"

My eyes were locked on the pamphlet in my hands. The girl that was modeling the uniform in the photograph was too pretty to believe.

"I never knew that girls like this really existed. I have to have her."

"Oh, come on. You know this isn't one of your games."

I had to come back to reality. She was just a model. It's not like she was really a student at the school, right?

It's like when you get fast food, and you see a picture of the hamburger you want, and it's the hamburger of your dreams, beautiful and perfect. So you order it, but what you actually get is nothing like the picture. It's smaller, uglier, and not as appetizing. That's just how the world works.

"Oh geez. Now I really want a teriyaki burger."

I must have been thinking out loud. And it seems I'd made Shigure really hungry—not that I cared.

"That girl in the picture is the headmaster's

granddaughter. She's a second-year student this year."

Right, right. Go buy a hamburger then. Oh, and will you get some nuggets for me?

"WHAT!? Can you say that again!?"

"I really want a teriyaki burger."

"Not that!"

"I'm the representative of the Manga Research Club."

"You really had to reach for that one, didn't you!? It's still not what I meant!"

"That girl in the picture is the headmaster's granddaughter. She's a second-year student this year."

Good God.

It was a divine revelation! It had to be! My destiny was as clear as day. I'd enroll at the academy and meet her. Then we would fall madly in love, only to end up stalked by the photographers of the Newspaper Club. We'd call a meeting for all the reporters, during which we would have to endure slander (that sprang from their secret jealousy). Everything would end up fine and all of them would end up wishing us their best. Then a few years would go by and we would get married. Then we'd have two children (both girls), whose names would be . . .

"Um, Eruna-chan?"

"I made up my mind."

"You know that two girls can't get married, right?"

"That's not what I meant! I mean I've decided to take the entrance exam for this academy."

My mood had completely turned around. I found myself humming a song as I flipped through the rest of the pamphlets.

"You know the entrance exam isn't exactly easy."

I wasn't paying Shigure any attention. I was concentrated on cutting out the picture of my dream girl and trying to find just the right picture frame for it.

"Heh, heh. It's all going according to plan," Shigure whispered to himself, but my cackling and shrieking drowned him out.

*

Studying for the entrance exam took all the free time I had.

I bought some reference books and started studying so hard that all the weeks I'd been relaxing for up until that point felt like a distant memory. Every day, I learned and memorized more and more. I cut into my sleep time to cram in more study time. And whenever I wasn't studying I was practicing diligently for the interview.

Okay, that might have been a slight exaggeration. Okay, maybe it was just a flat-out lie. I didn't really buy reference books; I bought some yuri manga and committed to my lazy life even more than before. Instead of stuffing my head, I filled my belly with as many snacks as I could. I had no way of figuring out when I'd gotten sufficient sleep, so I stayed in bed for as long as I could. I completely forgot that there would even be an interview after the exam.

That's not all. Neglecting any responsibilities that come with being a young woman at my age, I stopped brushing and washing my hair until it was a tangled mess. I told my mom that it was the latest fashion and that it was just too cool for her to understand. I think I lost my chance to convince her that I was on top of things when she realized I never changed out of my pajamas until late in the evening.

"Of course I wouldn't tell you this directly, but I kind of hope that you move into the dorms soon."

"You wouldn't tell me directly!? You're talking right into my ear! I can hear everything you're saying!"

"That must be our strong mother-daughter connection. You understand my thoughts without even having to hear them. I wonder if you could tell I was angry about that cake that went missing? The one I'd been saving in the refrigerator?"

Whoops! Yeah, I probably shouldn't have done that. After the cake had disappeared, we both stood there looking at the empty spot on the refrigerator shelf, and I think I'd said, "There must be a ghost!"

I guess I hadn't managed to fool her.

So days passed uneventfully, marked only by my mother's occasional frustrated pleas for our ghost to return her beloved cake.

Soon enough, the day of the test came.

I consider it a talent of mine to never get too worked up over things. Friends in the neighborhood had taken to saying that, whenever we agreed to meet at a certain time, they would come an hour late. That was when I could be expected to show up. All I could do was giggle at their jokes, because they were right. I'd adopted a decidedly relaxed attitude regarding time commitments. So you see it really wasn't out of character for me to sleep in nice and late on the day of the exam.

"C'mon, mom! Why didn't you wake me up!?"

I didn't even have time to get dressed. I thought about taking the test in my pajamas just to make sure my mother understood how severely she had inconvenienced me. I pressed her on the point, but I had to admit defeat.

"I tried to wake you up, but you moaned that the exam time had been changed, so that you could sleep later if you wanted to."

First I was annoyed. Then I found myself pausing for a moment in surprise. The emotion train continued on to speechlessness and kept right on going until I had no idea where I was anymore.

Sigh . . . I suppose it was my fault for telling a bald-faced lie to stay in bed. Shame on me. Forgive me, mother! The train kept right on going, and I ended up lost.

There were a bunch of different rooms for the entrance exam, and based on where you were applying from, you were assigned a room. It looked like I was the only applicant from my neighborhood.

Back in middle school, my homeroom teacher had been a 27-year-old single woman who always said that she hated to round things up. When we'd had a private conference about my plans for continuing education past middle school, she didn't ask about my plans at all or tell me anything about how the application process would proceed. However, she did ask, "Do you know of any rich bachelors in your neighborhood?"

Her bloodshot eyes aroused my sympathy, so I humored her. You see, I'm really a very kind person at heart. Granted, I might eat my mother's cake in secret, but I'm really a good person on the inside! "Hmm . . . well what kind of salary do you want this bachelor to have?"

"Five and a half million . . . actually I better round that up to ten million. Hey, don't make me round things up! I'll see to it that you're expelled! I swear it!"

"Are you out of your mind? I'm about to graduate!"

She was rounding up too much, and it was ruining the conversation. How greedy can you be?

I remembered that weird conversation with my old teacher as I ran desperately around like a fool, praying that no one would recognize me later.

The campus was huge, a small town of its own. I climbed to the top of a tower that offered a good view of the campus from above. When I got to the top, I was drenched with sweat, but I was greeted with a view of expansive western-style buildings.

At the entrance to one of the buildings stood a woman whose entire being and atmosphere said, "I'm a maid."

Without thinking, I hopped over to her and shouted, "Hey there, Ms. Maid, you're looking a little bummed out, but I love maids! Mind if I take a picture!?"

I rummaged desperately through my bag.

I didn't have a camera. I suppose I'd forgotten it at home. I suddenly realized that I'd bought the camera for this very moment, and now its true destiny would go unfulfilled. Life is cruel.

"Hey, do you mind if I run home to grab my camera?"

"You must be Eruna Ichinomiya. The preparations for your entrance exam are all ready. Right this way please."

She completely ignored me. What a professional!

Argh . . . I could tell that I was blushing. It was embarrassing to be ignored so completely.

The maid, who from what I could tell was the same

age that I was, didn't wait for me to answer. She turned and forcefully led me into the building.

How cool and beautiful. What a cool, beautiful mirage!

So I just decided to call her Kurumi-san*.

Sometimes people say that I'm not good at coming up with nicknames—that there's a destructive, pessimistic edge to the things I come up with. They are totally WRONG. It's just that my genius is the sort that won't get recognized until years after I die. It's just a little too *advanced* for your average folks.

That's fine by me. I don't need everyone's approval. Those that get it get it.

. . . So far no one in my life has gotten it.

Feeling like I was trapped in a cold, uncompromising situation, I was seized by the sudden compulsion to do something about it. I had to improve things. I had to build bridges, not walls!

"Kurumi-san, have you been working here very long? Are you in a relationship? If not, what do you think about me? Ahaha! Just kidding!"

"Your written examination will take place in this room here. Please have a seat and wait for the test to be administered."

". . . Alright."

I could nearly hear my heart breaking in my chest.

Eruna-chan, you've learned something important today.

I looked around the room and discovered that it was way too big for just one person to take a test in. The walls were covered in tasteful art. Fine pieces of pottery stood on display here and there. It felt like the room was screaming at me, "I'm rich! Don't you get it? RICH!"

I felt like a bumpkin from Fukui prefecture, stepping off the train in Tokyo for the first time, eyes wide and fascinated by everything. Not that I have a problem with people from Fukui! I just thought it was appropriate for the simile.

"Hm . . . Is this painting the work of the impressionists?"

Sometimes, if I know that no one can hear me, I pretend to appraise artwork. Of course I don't actually know anything at all about impressionism. I just like hearing myself say things like that.

"And look at this pot! The aesthetic is marvelous!"

I shouted, pointing at a pot. I don't even know what "aesthetic" means.

I couldn't think of any other way to appraise the objects in the room, so I continued, "It looks like you couldn't break it if you tried!" I figured that was vague enough that no one would question it.

Then I realized that the pot I was complimenting was actually a flower vase, so I clapped my hands once and struck all that I'd said from the record. That was enough—I'd gotten over my compulsion to appraise the room, so I finally took my seat in silence.

I just sat there, slack-jawed, looking like a fool until Kurumi-san (yes, I'd already made up my mind that that was going to be her name) came over to my desk with the test.

It appeared that she was also going to be acting as the test administrator.

I'd finally realized that she was going to ignore me if I kept trying to start a conversation, so I decided it was time to abandon my dream of building bridges and devote myself to actually taking the test.

Eruna-chan, it must be said, does not like to be ignored. I, normally, break down crying. No, more like, if I get attention, I turn into a little animal that wags her tail so hard she breaks things. Sorry if that sounds like I'm bragging.

I took a peek at the packet of questions and the provided answer sheets. Then I steeled myself to jump into the exam head-first. I could hardly believe my eyes.

The questions were too easy. They were so easy, in fact, that I was sure I must have been given the wrong test.

I looked over to Kurumi-san and signaled with my eyes, as if to say, "Are you sure this is it?"

"That's it," she seemed to say by affirmatively nodding her cute little chin.

Really?

Maybe I'd accidentally gone to the wrong school? Like, maybe I wasn't at Mikagura Academy, but Mikagura Kindergarten?

Of course, I wasn't about to point out their error and just head home.

And besides, hadn't she called me by name and led me to the test room?

"What is the deal with this test?"

A generous 50 minutes had been provided for the first section. I'm not exaggerating when I say that it was so easy I could have completed it in one minute.

For whatever reason, I wasn't able to just be happy

about it and count my blessings—I'd look like a psycho if I sat there smiling to myself. Granted, I had forgiven myself for my eccentricities long ago, but the questions on the test were making me doubt my sanity again.

I started overthinking things and ended up even more confused than I should have been. When I saw an easy question, I wondered if it was some kind of trap. Maybe I had to hold the paper up to a light to see the REAL questions, like they'd been scrawled in invisible ink or something!

I closed one of my eyes and held the paper up the light to check it out.

Then I let my eyes flit over to Kurumi-san to see what she thought of my strange behavior. Just like before, she didn't respond at all. She didn't even look in my direction!

"Maybe I need to hold it up to a flame to make the secret writing appear!?"

"Oohhhh stfwwwaaaapid . . ." Kurumi-san yawned so dramatically that she must have done it on purpose.

The end of her yawn sounded like she was calling me stupid. I'm sure I was just imagining things. It was just your normal, everyday yawn, right? I had to discard my suspicions. All real relationships were built on trust, right? Isn't that how it works?

I spent the vast majority of my allotted time looking for secret traps that I assumed had been encoded into the questions, wearing myself out in the end. I finished the test. I was more tired than I should have been.

"I didn't find anything strange. It was just a written test. So why do all my muscles ache?"

I overthought everything to the point where I'd convinced myself that I was the victim of some complicated scheme. In the end, I tried turning the test upside down, but I only succeeded in rendering the whole thing unintelligible.

Sometime around the middle of my allotted time, Kurumi-san seemed to stop worrying about me at all. From what I could tell, she'd started napping. I decided to pretend that I was imagining things—she had no reason to ignore me!

She looked very sleepy, and she yawned again, "Fwwaaaaiew ahs oooooooxt."

"What was that!?"

"The interview is next. Follow me," she repeated herself in the same disinterested tone and led me down a hallway on sleepy, tottering legs.

Was she . . . alright? Was this academy okay? What had I gotten myself into?

I kept my insecurities private as she led me deeper into the center of the building.

The building itself was enormous, but it didn't look like anyone lived there.

It almost felt like a hallucination, like I'd wandered into the place in a dream. It wasn't a bad feeling at all. To be honest, I loved it! I couldn't help but love it.

"Here we are."

Those words cut through my wandering thoughts and my fantasy popped like a bubble. After all, my cousin Shigure had told me time and time again how trying the interview process was.

On the night before I decided to apply to the academy, Shigure turned to me with a big smile plastered over his face and said, "Eruna-chan, how about we practice for the interview?"

There was only one reasonable answer to a question like that. "No way, it's a waste of time!" Sure enough, he looked like he was about to burst into tears at that, so I had no choice but to entertain his interview game.

Ever since I was little, Shigure had liked me a little too much for comfort.

It was especially obnoxious on Valentine's Day. He'd follow me around incessantly until I eventually caved in and accepted whatever present he'd made me that year. I can't help mention this one particular Valentine's Day.

"Heeey! I bet you know what day it is!"

"I don't."

"Ugh! Sweets! All of a sudden, I feel like I'm going to die if I don't get my hands on something sweet!"

"Go ahead and die then."

"I wanted to lend some gravitas to today's events, so I drew a manga about it!"

Shigure was part of the Manga Research Club, and he'd started drawing manga that featured me as the protagonist. Of course he never asked for my permission.

I took a deep breath to steady myself before asking, with hesitation, "And what sort of manga have you drawn this time?"

Years of experience had taught me that he would only get more persistent and obnoxious if I didn't indulge him.

"Huh? You want to know? You want to see it, don't you?"

"Ugh! You are so annoying!"

"How dare you! I can hear it in your voice! You don't want to see it at all, do you!?"

Whoops. I'd made my disgust a little too evident.

He looked hurt. I glanced over at the manga as he grandiosely displayed each page. I couldn't bring myself to hate it completely.

I couldn't avoid him forever. So eventually, I always caved in and gave him what he wanted.

We were related and sometimes he pushed too hard with his familiarity. But still, I had to admit that a part of me was probably pretty fond of him. Of course, I would never tell him that—he'd lose his mind in sheer ecstasy if I did.

"Okay, so what kind of manga did you draw this time?"

"It's a love story set on Valentine's Day. It's the story of a forbidden love that blossoms between a boy and his cousin!"

"On second thought, maybe you really should go ahead and die."

I couldn't let him get away with writing a manga like that. No way. No how.

I had to completely, unequivocally, and masterfully avoid getting entangled in his stupid manga any further!

Flipping through it, there was a danger of being tricked by a perfunctory examination, because the manga was full of attractive, cool girls. So why did he insist on drawing me like . . .

My head hung as I flipped through it, which he seemed to misinterpret as a nod of approval, because he launched into an unsolicited explanation.

"The story starts from the perspective of a young girl who cannot help but fall in love with her cousin, who is attractive and intelligent. His character is pretty much unassailable."

He spoke in a lilting singsong voice, clearly thrilled by his story. Then he would pause and wink at me, as if to say, "Don't you want to know what happens next?"

"Hi-yaaah!" I shouted, and forcefully ripped the manga from his hands before tearing it into pieces.

"Wh . . . What are you doing!?"

He collapsed and held his head in his hands. I watched him without a shred of guilt. What further injustices would I suffer if I indulged him with tacky sympathy now?

I couldn't wait to see how he reacted, with his precious manga in smithereens.

"Oh well, I have plenty of copies!" he said, leaping to his feet and pulling a stack of manga from somewhere and dropping it on the table top with an impressive *slam!*

It was a mystery to me. How could this nightmare keep going? It was starting to hurt my head just thinking of a way out of it. Of course, I already knew the answer.

There was only one path out of this madness. It was fraught with danger. But I didn't have any other choice.

"Fine. I'll give you a little."

"Oh yay! Thanks again, Eruna-chan!"

I gave him a few pieces of chocolate, cursing myself for even setting any aside for him. I suppose a part of me liked playing into his hands.

Just thinking about it made me dizzy.

As a general rule, he didn't really listen to anything you said after he initiated a conversation.

His insistence on practicing for my interview would probably follow the same pattern.

"Eruna-chan. Let's practice for your interview."

He smiled at me again.

When I let my actual emotions slip out and told him that I didn't want to, he hadn't minded. He just brushed it off and kept going, which meant I wasn't going to get out of it. And if I wasn't going to get out of it, then any effort I expended trying to escape would only tire me out in the end. I had to submit to get it over with.

I set my cheek down on my fist to make my impatience clear, hoping he would get the point, and yawned, "Fine. Let's get this interview going."

"First things first, you'll never make it through the interview with an attitude like that! If you introduce yourself that way, you'll be disqualified in a heartbeat! Remember, applying to schools is a war, and the other students are your opponents. If you slip beneath the waves, you're a goner!"

"What!?"

I pursed my lips and made my distaste evident, shooting him a nasty look that amounted to "well if the interview is over then I guess I'll just be on my way!"

He went on. "Eruna-chan lost the great application war and then lost her way in life. She lost sight of her goals, she lost her family, herself, her emotions! Eventually, she walked the night streets in a daze, only to be saved by me, at which point she remembered her true self, her true nature, and then we lived happily ever after."

"Yikes! That was terrifying! What!? No! What happened to my family and to my emotions? All that because I failed a test? And you know, to be honest, the happy ending rang a little hollow—don't you see that would be a tragedy for my character?"

He only answered by making a face that seemed to say, "What are you freaking about? You know it's cute!"

What was I supposed to do? It was too much . . . I couldn't handle it by myself . . . I never wanted to see him in the first place. I never even wanted to be in his presence . . .

Apparently he could see how upset I was, so he snapped to attention, smiled, and continued. "Very well then, why don't we try it again? From the beginning? I'll ask the questions."

He sat there pretending to stroke a beard that (of course) he didn't actually have and recommitted himself to what must have been the performance of his life: the interview administrator.

"Your interview administrator for the day has, thankfully, lived a long life (88 years!). He is currently upset that his granddaughter refuses to eat his beef stroganoff, a recipe he devoted years to perfecting."

My interest had been sitting at a solid zero. That backstory pushed it into the negative range. But I admit that negative numbers are kind of interesting.

For starters, why would an interview administrator be so old? He played the character blinking very slowly, which made me think that maybe he'd died each time his eyes closed. And besides, why was his granddaughter so rude about the stroganoff? And—maybe this isn't the best time to bring it up—isn't "beef stroganoff" kind of fun to say?

I had so many protestations I wanted to say that I got overwhelmed and ended up just sitting there in silence, a little out of breath. There was no need to give up completely. If I wanted out, the easiest way out might be cooperation. I waited for his questions.

"Eruna Ichinomiya-san, you have a nii-chan, dontcha?"

"I do NOT!"

And you know what else? If he was going to insist

on this elderly administrator character, he should stop saying things like "dontcha." He sat there wiggling slightly, like he could hardly hold himself up. Was this old guy okay?

When I answered in the negative, Shigure nodded solemnly to himself and continued, "Even though he's not your nii-chan, don't you have a cousin that you love very deeply?"

"I don't know about love. I have a cousin that I try my best to *avoid*."

"Ugh."

He clutched his chest as if he'd been stabbed through the heart, and his eyes filled with tears.

Success! Heh, heh. Shigure pulled at his imaginary beard (I guess he kept that part of the character intact) and used it to wipe his tears away. He kept clearing his throat and coughing dramatically, to make sure he kept the old-man illusion up. Finally, he collected himself enough to continue.

"Mikagura Academy houses its students on campus, in dormitories. The students are not permitted to return to their family homes without explicit permission from the headmaster or the head of the student committee.

Knowing that, what would you do if that cousin of yours suddenly fell ill?"

"Huh? Oh, I don't know. Throw a party?"

"You'd celebrate instead of worrying? And could you please stop smiling that way, as if you've finally articulated the point you came here to make!? You're smiling like the clouds have finally parted! And what a smile! I can almost hear the light flashing off of your pearly whites!"

"Boo . . ." I frowned to let him know I didn't approve of his direction.

Shigure discarded the geriatric character and got serious, taking a moment to settle his nerves before continuing. I suddenly realized that this whole charade was probably a calculated effort to relax me before the interview.

Granted, I didn't have the sort of personality that left me tied in anxious knots all the time, but if he went out of his way to relax me, then I was grateful for the effort.

I felt a little happy. So I must have let myself smile just a little. He tipped his head to the side, watching me closely, and said, "Maybe I should force you into a serious interview and use the opportunity to plant subliminal messages about myself? No, that could backfire. Better I just be my warm, kind self, and those feelings will develop on their own."

"Dream on!"

"No? Oh, so I guess I'm wrong!?"

He shook his head violently and pressed the issue further. For some reason he'd developed a Kansai* accent in the process. What happened to the elderly administrator? The new guy was stressing me out.

The situation had become too stifling to enjoy anymore, and any semblance there had been to an actual admissions interview was long gone.

So I'd gotten the idea that the interview was going to be particularly arduous. Shigure had made me feel that way. Under the auspices of his pseudo-charity, he'd pretended to help me prepare, only to act like an idiot and cause me to trust him even less than I already had.

So how did I feel going into the interview, knowing that I'd practiced all I could? Had I just imagined it? Was my confidence the result of a hallucination? They say that you reap what you sow, so maybe I felt powerless because I hadn't put in much effort. I decided to observe the maid, Kurumi-san.

"Oh, um . . . Kurumi-san. You smell so . . . so good . . ."

I sniffed at the air.

"To try and capture it in words . . . well . . . It's like the sweet smell of a fully ripe melon, just on the verge of rotting."

Nothing!

I'd tried to pay her the most poetic compliment I could think of, but she just stared at me in silence. It was terrifying.

All I'd wanted to do was emphasize the fruity complexity, the sublime scent, on the air. I didn't mean to . . . to . . .

I suddenly realized I was standing there running the scene over and over in my mind without explaining myself. Kurumi-san stepped towards a door and motioned mechanically.

"This. Is. The. Room."

She made her irritation clear by forcefully enunciating each word. Had my compliment really been bad enough to warrant that much anger? *Fine then!* I'd just do what she said, if that's what she wanted.

I pushed against the thick, oppressive door and it

slowly swung open to reveal a room so full of light that it stung my eyes.

"What the!?"

Before I could even get my hands up to cover my eyes, I felt an authoritative shove from behind, and I had no choice but to walk into the room. It was still too bright to open my eyes, and the door slammed shut behind me before I could get a sense of my surroundings.

"I have to do the interview blind!? Isn't that a little *experimental*?"

I was sure that wasn't the case. I couldn't just stand there in silence while I waited for my eyes to adjust.

What if it really was a blind interview? How should I have responded? They were probably looking for confident posturing, so maybe I should have struck a pose and shouted, "I can see just fine!" I wasn't sure if I'd be a good fit for a school that expected so much.

"I . . . I can see just fine!"

I tried saying it anyway, just to cover my bases. I was as serious as I could muster.

I had to do my best if I wanted to meet that girl! Sometimes we must suffer if we want to achieve greatness.

I felt like I should probably be able to open my eyes by then, so I slowly tried to open them. And then—

"... What?"

It was like I'd imagined all the light. When I opened my eyes the room was just an ordinary room.

The only source of light was an ornate lamp in the corner.

For a room with such a huge door, the reality failed to live up to what I'd imagined. Far from being an expansive hall, it was just an average, small room. There was little furniture or furnishings, giving it a somewhat desolate appearance that was offset by the bold and elaborately patterned wallpaper.

I looked around the room to get a sense of what was going on and found a single chair set in the center of the space. I assumed they expected me to take a seat and wait. There was no table provided, as if they hadn't felt that someone of my standing was worthy of one.

I stole another glance back at the entrance, only to find the door firmly shut.

The silence was oppressive to the extent that I could hear the ringing in my ears and the pounding of my heartbeat, which had started to take on a samba-esque beat.

Okay, maybe I oversold that a little. It wasn't really a samba beat. That was an exaggeration.

But my point stands. Something about the room made me unspeakably nervous.

Unsure of what to do next, I stood there blinking for a moment or two.

"Is anyone here?"

I hadn't seen any sign of an interview administrator yet.

They were probably on their way.

"This little one doesn't seem to have it, ryui."

I heard a small voice come from somewhere above me, so I rushed to find the source. There was a bizarre creature floating in the air above me. It was unlike anything I'd ever seen before.

"Ryui! She is definitely an Ichinomiya and she doesn't have any siblings. Truly, and literally, one of a kind. It's very rare to be born with so little ability though. We even went out of our way to prepare that test specifically for her, so this is a shame. Such is life, ryui."

It looked like a cat with wings but also a bit like a

dog. It was a strange-looking little monster. It crossed its arms and looked down at me, like it was deep in thought, and muttered to itself the whole time.

Was it a stuffed animal? Something radio-controlled? A robot, maybe? Whatever it was, it was so well-made as to be thoroughly convincing, and I was impressed.

I looked at the weird thing from different angles, trying to figure out what it could be. It kept floating there and muttering to itself. I decided to try poking it. Then I gave it a little pat on the head. It was so soft and warm!

It didn't respond to my prodding at all. I tried jabbing it in the eye with my finger.

"Hi-ya!"

"Ahhhh! Ryui!"

Finally, it responded. It wasn't very reactive. Whoever had made it had done a real bang-up job. I was sure it must have been a scientist of some sort. He probably worked in solitude for years, twirling his manicured mustache while he tried to perfect the cuteness of his creation. I'm sure he'd been a passionate figure, but I wasn't sure this whole "ryui" thing was a good idea.

I nodded to myself, impressed, and closely observed the way it responded to stimulation.

"So the eyes are its weak point . . . I see . . . I'm going to try pulling its wings off next."

The little thing just went on screaming as the beautiful young girl (me!) moved to attack it.

"S . . . Stop it, ryui! Just listen to what I have to say, ryui!"

"Huh?"

"What a cruel child, ryui! How could you act with violence towards cute, lovely little me?"

It flapped its little wings and flew madly around the room.

It seemed to think it, itself, was cute. But to be honest, something about it didn't sit well with that descriptor. What adjective would be more appropriate? Ugly? Maybe a little half-baked?

"I bet you're thinking all sorts of rude things, ryui!"

Could it read minds? Could it really be so powerful? Then again, people always tell me that I wear my emotions on my sleeve. My face probably gives my thoughts away.

Anyway, there was a more immediate question to

contend with. Just what WAS the thing?

"I'm △×●■◆! A member of the private Mikagura Academy, ryui! I've been entrusted with conducting the interviews today, ryui!"

The little monster announced its name, but it was too complicated to remember.

And it's rude to ask someone to repeat their name, isn't it? How best to navigate these treacherous waters? I know! I'll make up a nickname to smooth things over. Good idea Eruna-chan! Yup, everything would be smooth sailing . . .

I am kind of a genius when it comes to nicknames, after all.

"Well, your face is a little weird, so how about I call you Bimii*? How's that?"

"How's that? It's terrible, ryui! Don't ever call me that, you rude girl!"

"I know you probably say 'ryui' like that because you think it makes your character more interesting, but it really doesn't match your voice well at all! I think you should give it up."

His voice was sonorous and manly, so that cute little "ryui" didn't feel like it fit. The voice made me assume that the little thing was male, but these days not even the tackiest gyaruge* featured male characters with little catchphrases like that. It just didn't feel balanced.

"Oh, really, howawa? Does this fit me better, howawa?"

Howawa? A cold shiver ran down my spine. Maybe it was so bad that it was good? No, no—of course it wasn't. I should come to my senses before making any hasty decisions. I tried thinking really hard about it, and then I tried to completely empty my mind and approach it fresh. Nothing helped—no matter how I approached it the new catchphrase just seemed worse.

I shot an annoyed glance at him and shook my head. He thought for a while before responding pathetically, "Then what do you think would fit my character? Will you tell me, ryui?"

"Hmm . . . That's a good question."

It was easy enough to find fault. Faced with the task of inventing something new, I had to admit it was difficult. Obviously, I'd never given a catchphrase much serious thought. Thinking about it kind of felt sad in a way. Not only was I thinking about it, but I couldn't even come up with a good answer.

He was insistent that he was the interview administrator. I had to behave as though I were being evaluated. Someone really might have been watching us over a camera or something. What if it was all a test to see how I reacted?

I decided I better not chide the poor thing for much longer.

It was staring at me expectantly, as if to say, "I might be a little ugly, but my eyes are pretty and I'm full of spunk!"

He was just making it harder on himself!

I don't think anyone had ever looked at me with such innocent, expectant eyes before, not even once! The fact filled me with a tender sadness, as if I suddenly saw how empty all my years had been—there was no sense in dwelling on it! I decided to just say whatever popped into my head.

"What if you said 'busa' for your catchphrase? It's full of originality!"

"It certainly has an individualistic quality to it, busa. There's an originality to it that will help me stand out, busa." He nodded his approval then suddenly lit up as if he'd realized something. "But wait a second! Did you just come up with that because you think I'm ugly? And what if a sentence ends with 'de' and I end up saying 'debusa*!?' I'm not fat or ugly, busa!"

Bimii was flapping hard around the room, like he couldn't believe the situation he was in. He may have had catchphrase issues, but I had to admit that he was kind of fun.

"You say things like 'bimii' and 'busa' . . . Why are you so mean, ryui?"

"So we're back to 'ryui' now, are we? Fine, it's cute enough! Are you a little angel!?"

"You can't pay me compliments now! I can see your little half-smile! This is all a joke to you, isn't it?"

There I went, wearing my emotions on my sleeves again.

I guess I'm not so good at keeping secrets. I can't really lie either. Eruna-chan is a champion of justice who shares the truth of her heart with others!

"Am I puffing myself up too much, ryui?"

"Can you try to stay positive?"

That was probably my greatest asset—my ability to stay positive, no matter the circumstances! Sometimes I get a sarcastic well-aren't-you-a-ray-of-sunshine response. In the end, I think I have a way of charming others.

Ah! Smiles should always follow smiles. Life should be an unbroken chain of smiles!

"Then maybe you could treat me as if you wanted me to smile too, ryui."

Bimii frowned.

"Well, sometimes these things happen."

"And whose fault is that, ryui!?"

When he got angry like that he flapped around madly, and it was kind of cute.

It was just *kind of* cute though. Unfortunately, I couldn't get rid of that modifier in good conscience.

I crossed my arms and tried to settle down. It was time to get serious.

I came into the room to have my interview. That's when Bimii came and declared himself the administrator.

Whenever I looked over at the flying creature, it returned my gaze, as if to ask what I wanted.

At first, I'd thought that the thing was a piece of art or a robot of some kind. But watching the way it spoke, and the jokes it told, I realized that couldn't be the case. I tapped my finger against its wiggly cheek as I considered it.

"Stop that, ryui! It tickles, ryui!"

"Could you please just breathe normally?"

The thing had been taking hard, ragged breaths, and now it was blushing.

Bimii's voice was clearly that of an adult male, so I couldn't help but find this new reaction of his a little unsettling.

Everything it said felt like what you'd expect a little creature to say, but the voice just didn't fit. It was awkward.

"Did God make a mistake when he put you together? Was there some kind of slip-up?"

"Hey now! There you go again! I can tell you really feel that way, ryui! I have a life, too, and I was born into this world like just like anyone else. Life is sacred, not a mistake! More like a *takeoff*, ryui!"

I wasn't sure what he meant about "takeoff."

Was he going somewhere?

"Was takeoff the wrong word, ryui? Um ... *takeout*?"

Or maybe someone was going to take him home after dinner? I'm probably the last person alive who should say something like this, but I was getting the impression that my new friend wasn't very smart.

Not that it mattered, but how long were we going to keep going back and forth? I really wanted to finish the interview as soon as possible so I could go home, eat snacks, and do nothing for the rest of the day. I was starting to get impatient.

Bimii was flying in circles over my head, so I reached out and grabbed him. "By the way . . ."

Once he was caught, Bimii immediately calmed down and put on a serious face. "That's right. I forgot to mention it. The interview results have already been posted, ryui!"

Suddenly, the conversation was back on track.

"What do you mean the interview results are already posted? Did we even start yet?"

I couldn't remember anything we'd discussed since I entered the room that even remotely resembled a formal interview. Actually, come to think of it, I don't think I'd made a single constructive comment since I'd arrived. That couldn't be good. A jolt of desperation shot through me.

I must have failed. If this was the interview, then I definitely failed it!

If the interview was based on my attitude, or on the topics I brought up in conversation, then I would be disqualified for sure! Or maybe there could be multiple outs, maybe even lots of them? Maybe the interview process was more like baseball? If I was the pitcher, I'd want to get as many outs as I could. But what if I was the batter? If so, then . . .

"This is my chance to turn the whole thing around!"

"Little overoptimistic, aren't you, ryui?"

He made a little annoyed face that was just as weird and malformed as everything else he did. I really wanted to turn my back on him, and I really wanted to scream my disagreement. He kept flying in circles over my head. The first time around I cocked my head to the side in confusion. The second time I held him in suspicious regard. By the third time he came around I finally accepted it, feeling all my combative energy drain away.

He was a little ugly, but he was also a little cute. I'd have to call him "ugute."

I nodded to myself, trying it out silently. Yes, it worked. That decided it! He probably wouldn't like it too much if I let him in on my thoughts though.

"What is it? Are you thinking of rude things to say again, ryui!? Just stop already!"

He took a deep breath and leveled his eyes at me as if to say, "Now I have an important announcement to make."

It annoyed me a little. I steadied myself and tried not to overreact. I imagined a menu popping up inside my head, like in an RPG battle, and I selected the quietly-listen-like-an-adult option.

I should point out that I didn't get this idea of RPG battles because Bimii looked like a monster. It wasn't like that at all. Nope, not a bit . . . right?

I sat there savoring my inner conflict when Bimii announced, "After your interview performance, Mikagura Academy has decided to enthusiastically accept your application! Taken together with the results of your written examination, we would be honored if you accepted admission to our institution!"

"Why!?"

It was too easy, too simple, too unbelievably smooth! How had they decided? It was only natural that I respond in the interrogative.

"You can ask why all you want, but you've passed

with flying colors, ryui! Furthermore, your scores put you near the top of your class, ryui!"

"What's with this place!?"

It was so easy that I started to worry.

I hadn't given it a lot of thought yet. Still, I couldn't help but dwell on the fact that they had also admitted Shigure.

First they caught my eye with those cute uniforms. Then they stole my heart with a picture, until thoughts of the school sent me to a fantasy of blossoming flowers and friendships. I'd decided to apply easily enough, but what if . . . what if I'd set myself up for something really horrible!?

"It's okay, ryui! I guarantee your admission, ryui! Welcome to the academy. Let's set sail on a ship of knowledge and imagination, ryui!"

"Oh, don't you worry about me! I have a feeling that ship is going to sink any minute now!"

He'd even said that I was near the top of my class. What could that have meant? I'm not bragging of course, but I hadn't been near the top of my class since the second grade.

Back then, everyone had called me a genius and declared that I would either be a doctor or a politician.

My mother had been so proud. She imagined me working an important job and making a lot of money.

Ah, those were the days. Lately, her standards had dropped considerably. "Eruna-chan, it doesn't matter what you do for work. Whatever you choose is fine! Just please do something, anything!" She'd really lost hope.

That was how l came to learn that you could hurt people even with the best intentions and the nicest words.

"Anyway, your admission is real, ryui! Nothing to doubt! I'll see you at the entrance ceremony, ryui!"

Entrance ceremony? I couldn't help but picture it. I'd meet all the new girls there, and they'd all be dressed up in their fancy Mikagura Academy uniforms.

Then we'd go to the dorms, and I'd get to meet my roommate, who would have black hair, puppy dog eyes, and little boobs. Her name would be Yuriko. (Yeah, I know it's not the best nickname work I've ever done.)

"Yuriko? I'm going to turn the lights off, okay?" And then it would just be the two of us in the dark. In the silent darkness, the only sound would be our breathing. Our fingertips would accidentally brush against one another. "We shouldn't." Her whisper would float like silk curtains. "Either take off your clothes or mine, Yuriko . . ." "Who's doing who . . . Ah . . ." And then the two of us would inevitably fall—and fall hard—into a forbidden romance!

Yuriko!

Ahhhh! Yurikoooooo!

I'd let myself get lost in fantasy, only to have my daydream disturbed by the sharp, disinterested gaze of Bimii.

The gaze that tore my fantasy to shreds seemed to say, "What should we do with this trash? Throwing it away will be so much work . . . Can't someone come take it off our hands?" I might not me the most perceptive person in the world, but I could figure that much out.

"Um . . . As if . . . right?"

I did my best to put on a joking face and tried to gloss over my gaffe. The room had cooled down to absolute zero and I half expected a voice to come howling from the frost, saying, "Actually, we revoke that admission offer."

Then that RPG battle menu appeared in my mind again, and the only selectable command said "run away."

I silently made my selection, and before he could get a word in edge-wise, I turned my back on Bimii and made to run.

Before I dashed out of the room, I remembered that Bimii was supposed to be the interview administrator and I screamed, "Thank you very muuuuuuuuuch!"

I was pretty sure that my exclamation wasn't going to get me back any of the points I'd lost, but I figure it was worth a shot. If you're going to run out of a room, it's probably best to say "thank you" first.

"It seems like you couldn't pass a test to save your life. That is one of the reasons why I believe you will be a good fit for our academy, ryui," Bimii said softly as he watched me run from the room like a maniac.

"You passed the interview from the moment you were able to see me. Normally, I'm supposed to erase any memory you have of talking to me, before I send you home . . . "

I tried to shake my head to tell him no, when I heard another voice from outside the room.

"Oh, I don't think we have anything to worry about with her, ryui."

I looked behind me as I ran and saw Kurumi-san watching me leave. I smiled at her.

Her lips curled into a soft smile, one so slight that no one else could have seen it, and she nodded at me.

Okay, so I can't really remember much from the time I left the school until I made it back to my house. I just remember running, getting lost, falling down, and ruining my clothes. When I got home my mother shouted, "What the hell happened!?" I guess I looked very different than when I'd left that morning.

"I passed it! Easy! I'm a genius! Listen to this! You'll never believe it! The interview administrator was this weird creature named Bimii, and . . ." I went on for a little while like that, excitedly explaining all that had happened. My mother made a face like she finally understood something important, and she tenderly said, "You had a hard day, didn't you? You must be tired. Good for you, Eruna-chan, you really did your best! Why don't you go get some sleep? Go on now." And she forcefully dragged me over to my bed.

I lay down and she placed the blanket over me, pinching it carefully in the corner and making a face like she'd just hesitantly opened a jar of something really stinky. I suppose I shouldn't have expected her to believe me. I could hardly believe it all myself. It felt like a dream.

What if it really was a dream? If all of it had been a dream, if I was still in a dream now, then that meant I'd have to take the test all over again! No thank you! I was all out of HP and didn't know any resurrection spells.

But . . . But maybe the kiss of a true princess could restore me?

Ha! I guess I still had a little fight left in me. I smiled and slowly drifted off to sleep. I had dreams of the shining new school life I'd be starting and of the joyful future that awaited me. I believed in it all. There were no doubts remaining, not a cloud in the sky.

The official acceptance letter came in the mail a few weeks later.

In the spring, I would start new my life as a student at the private Mikagura Academy. The sky would celebrate with me, bluer than blue could be.

"Alright! Wait for me, shining youth! Wait for me, you beautiful babes!"

A light breeze carried my impure shrieks up into the purest blue sky I'd ever seen, gently, happily dissonant.

Just then, I thought I heard it: the sound of a new adventure beginning!

Movement Two: Hop Step Tornado

Eruna's placid mornings begin when the soft morning light filters in through the curtains.

She opens her eyes and a relaxed, crystal-clear smile spreads across her face, one so pure that you'd think she was on the set of a soft drink commercial. Her disheveled hair makes her easy to like, which is what commercial directors are always looking for.

She hears a small voice chirping "hurry, hurry!" and she decides to follow it. She pulls back the curtains from her canopy bed and softly steps out into her room.

The curtains are soft and white, like powder snow, and when she pulls them aside she sees a number of small birds waiting for her at the window. The chorus of their cheerful chirping is not meant to hurry her or to prod her along. No! They are simply stopping by to say good morning. Eruna leans down to deliver a morning kiss to each of them, after which they all open their little wings and take off to fly out to the town.

It was her morning routine, and she never missed

the opportunity to perform it, not even on her days off.

"Huh? Is she out there today?"

Eruna looked out her window to see a young girl, probably in middle school, gazing up at her window in hopes of catching a glimpse of Eruna.

Eruna waved to her cheerfully. That, too, was part of her new morning routine.

Whenever the younger girl realized that Eruna was waving to her, she blushed a bright red and took off running.

At breakfast, Eruna's mother mentioned the other girl. "That young girl was out there again today, was she? She must really like you," she said while she set the table with thick steaks and hummed a little song.

"Don't say that MOM!"

Eruna assumed that her mother was joking.

But her mother was probably right, considering the girl had once sent Eruna a love letter.

It had been sealed with a heart-shaped sticker, and the letter itself was full of naïve expressions of bittersweet love. Eruna had smiled when she read it.

So now, whenever Eruna caught sight of the girl in the morning, she tried to get her attention so she could thank her for the letter, at which point the girl would take off running. In truth, her skittish escapes were a little charming.

"Did I ever act like that?" Eruna opined, lifting a giant carrot-shaped stuffed animal into the air and addressing it. Wishing it would answer her, she twisted its face to approximate a nod.

Eruna liked the carrot's answer, so she buried her face in its body and hugged it tightly.

Eruna Ichinomiya was about to start her very first day at the private Mikagura Academy! It was time to get dressed up in that lovely uniform and become the graceful, demure girl that she was meant to be!

"I hope I meet a lot of really great people!"

As if to celebrate the first step into her new life, a colorful assortment of flower petals, carried on a fragrant breeze, floated past the window.

Eruna had woken up early, so she still had a lot of time to get ready. Naturally, she had already packed the bags that she would be taking to the dorm, but she went through them again just to confirm their contents. Then she thought it might be a good idea to take one last walk around her neighborhood.

She hummed a song as she slipped out of her pajamas and wondered if her little bird friends would come with her to the academy dorm. Then, as if they were telling her everything would be okay, the little birds chirped a beautiful song and flit around her window in excited spirals.

Everything was off to a perfect start! Her story was heading straight for happiness, and there were no obstacles to hold her back. Straight forward to the future!

"Straight forward to the future . . . um . . . munya."

Riiiiiiing! The alarm clock rang shrill, like the room could explode at any minute. Come to think of it, the clock's retail packaging had said, "This clock will wake anything up. No child can hold out. If you're human, this clock will wake you up." They'd designed the thing for people like me, people that can't ever seem to get out of bed. It was jumbo-sized.

My days start when I resolve to ignore the explosive sound of the clock as it shrieks by my bedside.

My curtains were thick. They featured the grinning face of a penguin character. I was fond of them, thinking they were a perfect example of the sort of unassailable womanly aesthetics I'd been born with. On the other hand, my friends all said they were awful because the smiling penguins were creepy, so who really knows? Anyway, the day starts when that awful, insistent, blinding light forces its way through the curtains and invades my sanctum.

I didn't give in. The light fell over my face, but I didn't move a millimeter. I'd realized that I could sleep through the light and the alarm clock if I incorporated those elements into my dream, which featured me in a security guard position.

If, for some reason, some director was forced to use me for their soft drink commercial, they'd have to settle on my sleeping face. Maybe they could zoom in on the dangling thread of spit that I made no effort to conceal. One thing was certain: their sales would suffer for it.

The room was filled with the explosive shrieking of the clock. To any outsider it would seem like the room had fallen into absolute chaos. It was an illustration of entropy that only made sense once you saw that disaster zone of my hair, so disheveled from my rambunctious sleeping patterns that it could never be tamed. Yup, if anyone saw my hair, they'd understand why my room was in the state it was in.

"You better shut up or you're not going to like what happens next!" I shouted at the noisy murder of crows that had started pecking around my window. They didn't respond to my threats, so I scrunched a penguin stuffed animal into a ball and threw it at them with all my might.

The crows weren't fazed when the penguin slammed against the windowpane. It was the same every morning. It was at the point where I could really just beg and plead for them the shut up and go away. Eventually they answered with a disinterested *caw* and flapped away to bother someone else.

The morning battle with the crows was part of my routine. It was so well known around the neighborhood that the little old ladies had started rumors about it. "If you want to keep the crows away, you have to get yourself an Eruna-chan!" they would say.

This probably goes without saying, but there were no cute little songbirds to greet me. I'd even heard rumors that the whole town had outlawed them.

"Eruna! Eruna!"

Someone was banging their fist against my window and calling my name.

"The entrance ceremony has already started, ryui! Wake up, ryui!"

I looked over at the clock to see that it was already pretty late in the morning. It was about time for normal people to start wondering what to do for lunch.

When I put my mind to it, I could be an ambitious over sleeper.

I dragged myself over to the window and wrenched it open so that Bimii could come in.

"What the . . . How . . . ?"

Bimii was stunned by the landscape he saw. It was one replete with dirty clothes, old manga, empty snack bags, and all other manner of trash. It was the sort of room you wouldn't be able to cross without stepping on something, even if you went on your tiptoes like a ballerina.

He was speechless. The alarm was still ringing. He turned the clock off and tried to get in a celebratory mood by jumping up and down on my bed.

"Wake up, ryui! Hey now! You better wake up, ryui! Get with it!"

I didn't want to be presumptive, but it looked to me like maybe jumping up and down was a higher priority than getting me out of bed. Maybe I was imagining it.

"Weeeeee! Ryui!"

He started to shout. It was the impassioned, frenzied shouts you'd expect from some barbarian living in a post-apocalyptic wasteland. He still kept that saccharine catchphrase of his. It really didn't suit him.

Realizing that I wasn't likely to respond to any sounds he made, he decided to jump on me physically by hopping onto my stomach with a heavy slam.

"Ugh!"

With each heavy bounce, he dragged me back into the world of the living.

"Eruna, your tummy is so bouncy! Bounce! Bounce! Flabby! Flabby! Ryui!"

Bimii seemed to have forgotten his original reason for coming. He was now devoting himself completely to playing with this new toy.

He looked so carefree, bouncing up and down in his innocent little Bimii way.

"Whose tummy is bouncy?? You little monster!"

"Ryui!? Keeee!"

I reared back and kicked him with a speed that impressed even me. He went flying and collapsed to the ground, twitching a little. He'd be fine, but I'd kicked him hard enough so that he knew I meant business.

"But I'm still sleeeepy! I've got an idea. Let's redefine 'morning' to mean whatever time I feel like getting out of bed. With it defined that way, that makes this the middle of the night."

I thought the suggestion was brilliant, but I hadn't managed to really wake up. I rubbed my sleepy eyes and said, "And how do you feel about making a fuss in the middle of the night? About robbing a young girl of her beauty sleep, eh, Bimii?"

Bimii smiled, came flapping over, and said, "You're talking nonsense, ryui. And are you really going to keep calling me Bimii? Can't I put in a request for a name change?"

"No, you may not! It fits you perfectly! Don't you get it!? There can be no better name. Besides, everyone knows that I have impeccable taste when it comes to naming things! Don't you think so, too? Don't you!?"

He looked at me like he didn't agree, so I just ignored him and started to dance by myself. I had to wake up somehow.

It was a very advanced dance. I unveiled it once during a dance class and the teacher praised me endlessly for it. He said that it looked like the kind of dance that would absorb magic points.

People had told me that my dance was so original that no one else could ever hope to pull it off. Tee-hee! I get embarrassed when people flatter me that way.

"Bimii . . . It's Bimii then, is it? After all I've done to serve as the academy's cutest mascot? After all the work I've put into crafting this immediately recognizable face? I fly around and everyone here knows me, but I guess to you I'm just Bimii . . . Oh well, ryui." He looked like he was about to burst into tears as he kept muttering his new nickname to himself.

I just couldn't believe that he thought he was cute. I thought about saying something, but thought better of it. Suppressing a yawn, I pulled open the curtains.

"Ah jeez. There he is, again."

I peeked out the window and saw him standing down in the street looking up at me, a boy with a shaved head and an obnoxious face.

When the boy noticed I had opened the curtains his whole face lit up, like an event he'd been waiting ages for had finally occurred. He fixed his eyes on me and narrowed them hatefully before jabbing his finger in my direction and shouting, "I've come to get my pii-chan back! You haven't eaten him yet, have you!?"

He was serious and screaming as loud as he could.

"What is he talking about, ryui?" Bimii asked, confused.

"If I explain it seriously it will just sound stupid. I've developed a reputation. The brats around here say I'm secretly a monster that catches little birds, fries them up, and eats them. Can you believe it? Why would a cute little girl like me do such a thing? I'd never, never, *never* fry a little birdie up! I love little birdies! I keep trying to get them to come to my window, but they never do!"

My rant grew more emotional as it went on. Bimii seemed to shrink back from me.

I don't normally wake up until just before lunch. I went in to talk to my mom at lunchtime and mentioned the rumors. All she had to say was, "Well, you don't look like someone that would eat anything. Like your mother's cake, for example." She was never going to let that one go.

Anyway, back to what's important! This kid had a

bird named pii-chan. The bird escaped one day while he was cleaning out its cage. Obviously, I had no idea where pii-chan had gone.

The little bird had probably relished its new freedom and gone to live peacefully in nature.

"Either that or he's found himself a new owner, a better owner!"

"WHHHHAAAT!? How dare you say that! Pii-chan would never do that to me!"

"Eruna, you really are heartless, ryui."

The boy burst into tears and took off running, swearing that he would be back tomorrow. I waved to him as he ran, thinking to myself that I'd never have to deal with him again, once I moved to the academy.

At least I'd be able to escape his unfounded suspicions. Wasn't this theory of his a little too disconnected from reality?

I'd had a dream that a cute girl was sending me love letters, but what did I get in reality? This boy hands me a chain letter that says if I don't mail out a hundred copies of the same letter within a week, I'd be cursed and get fat and die.

Ha! He could come up with whatever lies he wanted.

The dumb brat! I laughed it off, but I'd have to keep it secret. Near the end of the week, I had broken into a cold sweat before dutifully writing out a hundred copies of the letter. That was a secret I'd prefer to take to my grave.

In my defense, it had said that I'd get FAT and DIE. Just thinking of it terrified me beyond words.

I sighed heavily, like an overworked middle-aged man with a hangover, and searched for my giant carrot-shaped stuffed animal. Finding it in the corner, I held it aloft and delivered a quick series of punches to its carrot stomach.

I'd used the poor thing so often to relieve my stress that the stomach was wearing thin and had become permanently indented.

Regarding the giant carrot, Bimii said, "You just shattered any illusions I had about how young women behave, ryui."

His comment caught me off guard and I was left speechless. It was like he'd knocked the wind out of me!

Eruna Ichinomiya, this is your first day as a student at Mikagura Academy (but you're late)! Time to get all dressed up in your fancy new uniform (but you better change out of those ratty pajamas first)! Time to be cool and collected, the new girl at school (you just punched a giant carrot though)! The rest would happen just like it had in my dream.

"Here we go! Better get a little breakfast first!"

"Eruna, do you even understand what it means to be late, ryui?"

Outside of my window I caught sight of the buzzed-head boy stuffing another cursed letter into our mailbox—probably in an effort to bring more color to my brand new life.

Because I'd overslept, I didn't have time to chase him away. Even worse, I hadn't gotten prepared at all before I went to sleep the night before, so I would have to have my luggage sent to the school later.

It was a real skill I'd come to acquire. Remember, you can always do it tomorrow, and after tomorrow there will be another tomorrow! Future Eruna, you can do it!

My mother knows me pretty well though. Once I left the house, she'd rush in to clean behind me. I'm sure she'd pack up my stuff and have it sent along pretty quickly after that. I decided to take one last look around my room.

I'd spent so much time there since I was a small child. Now that it was time to leave, I found it harder to go than I'd expected. Every object in the room looked sparkling and magical to me. We'd formed a connection over years of living together.

Okay, that was all a lie. My room was disgusting, and everything in it looked like trash. I couldn't wait to get the heck out of there. Every object in the room had some kind of dark history.

I kept an eye on the clock as I changed out of my pajamas. The time indicated that I really was very late—too late to laugh it off. If ate my breakfast leisurely, I had a feeling my mother would really let me have it. I decided to skip breakfast altogether and just have a pouch of that jelly drink I like: Charge Up with Enough Energy for a Whole Year! Crazy Energy!

It was made by a small business in the neighborhood. It didn't list its ingredients at all. In the space where nutritional information is typically written, it said, "Who cares about this stuff? Get out there and WIN!" I couldn't argue with the results though. When I drank it, I actually felt so full of energy that I feared I might explode.

I whistled a little song while I tied the ribbon on my new uniform and wrapped my big puffy trademark scarf around my neck. I had picked my school based on this very uniform, so I took a minute to admire myself in the mirror. I was feeling pretty good. Then I noticed that everything in the mirror, aside from my well-executed outfit, was chaotic and trashy. I made up my mind to ignore it. Sorry, mom.

"Alright! Let's go!" I shouted at the top of my lungs and shot out of the house like a bullet, waving goodbye to my mother on my way out.

"I'll lead the way. You just stick with me, ryui!"

Bimii really wanted to take control of the situation, but I had to preserve my integrity. So I ran in the opposite direction that he indicated. My destiny was MINE to control! MY WAY!

"H . . . Hey! Don't ignore me like that! You think you're cool, but you're going the wrong way! Can't you hear me? That's mean, ryui!"

I patted his head and whispered softly to calm his nerves. "It was only a joke. There, there . . ."

The sun was blinding. I raised my hand to block the light.

This was the start of my new life. It was full of dreams and hopes (and plenty of alone time with cute girls). I was ready for it. I took off running (ready, set, go!).

I almost thought I heard the starting gun go off—it was probably just my own pounding heart.

I'd slept in and gotten a late start. Now I was running and all the lights were green!

Everything was perfect!

I kept my stride light and tried to enjoy the bouncing rhythm of my steps.

*

Wearing the uniform made me feel different, like a whole new life was waiting for me—or like I'd become an adult just by putting it on.

I knew it hadn't actually done any of those things. It was just a uniform, but I couldn't deny the effect that it had on my mood.

"Could it be you're in such a good mood because of that weird jelly drink, ryui?" Bimii asked doubtfully.

"How rude! That kind man at the shop wakes up

early every day so that he can craft that delicious masterpiece away from the eyes of those who might want to steal his secrets. It's a masterpiece, I tell you! A treasure!"

I sucked down more of the jelly as I ran. The nasty, muddy texture (its lumps slipped down my throat) was perfect for getting up and going in the morning.

"Actually, that secrecy makes me even more nervous, ryui."

The poor man had lost his wife, his daughter had gotten married and moved away, and now he ran the whole business by himself, despite being old and frail and suffering. Despite all his hardship, he'd developed this drink to help his young, sickly grandson Norio (I made that name up) make it through the day. After all his research and experimentation he finally perfected the recipe: Charge Up with Enough Energy for a Whole Year! Crazy Energy!

"Now Norio can run around the yard all he wants! He can curl up by the fire!"

Had I just mistaken his grandson for a dog or a cat? Whatever, Bimii probably wasn't listening anyway. I just had to say it with confidence.

"Now Norio comes by all the time, not just when he wants money or a new video game!"

His life was a lonely soliloquy until the day he perfected the recipe. When he knew that he had it right, he called up Norio's house and told them that he had a present for Norio.

"'Grandpa! Here I am!' yelled Norio when he ran into the house. Secretly, though, he planned to leave the minute he got his hands on the present."

"Well, well. Looks like my favorite cute little grandson hasn't learned what to say and what not to say."

Norio had run into the house without removing his shoes. He held both of his hands out and shouted "gimme, gimme!" The old man led him by the hand to the altar in the corner and kindly told him that he first had to say hello to grandma.

Norio dutifully paid his respects, after which the old man turned to him and said, "I've got a present for you, Norio! Look!"

And he passed the boy one pouch of Charge Up with Enough Energy for a Whole Year! *Crazy Energy!*

Norio, who was normally so frail, was filled with joy

and energy, and he smiled and shouted, "Thanks you, grandpa! Could this be . . . could this be . . . love?"

The boy was overjoyed, but he had confused his joy for the infatuation of romance.

"What do you think? Why not snap a picture and tweet it out to all your followers? I wonder what they would think of your grandpa's *Crazy Energy!* You should try it. Try tweeting it!"

Norio turned the package over carefully in his hands and inspected it before saying, "Okay, enough jokes. Where's the video game I wanted?"

His voice was suddenly mature, with a frigid bite to it. Without even the hint of a smile, he dropped the pouch of *Crazy Energy!* into the trash.

He tweeted, "It's no fun when the dentures play with your emotions."

Because the old man had often declared that Norio was so cute he could just eat him up, Norio had been calling his dear grandpa "dentures" in secret.

"The old man changed from that day on. He stopped washing his dentures. He hardly slept at all. He devoted all that he had to producing his *Crazy Energy!*"

"You've got an imagination alright, but isn't this getting a little long and dark, ryui?"

"Heh, heh."

I kept on running and immersing myself in the imagery of the strangely detailed drama that unfolded from the pouch of jelly in my hand. In doing so, I accidentally turned onto the wrong street and tripped. Everyone stared at me when I fell.

Luckily enough, I realized I'd fallen right in front of a bus stop that would take me right to where I wanted to go.

Of course, as I climbed to my feet, I discovered that the bus I needed to take had already left and there was no sign of it anywhere.

"Oh no! It's gone! It's moved so far away, just like Norio and his grandfather!"

"You have to let that fantasy go, ryui. I'm sure that Norio still cares for this grandfather, in his own way! He probably thinks of him all the time, ryui!"

Bimii suddenly looked like he would burst into tears. He must have really identified with the elderly jelly drink maker.

I was impressed by his ability to entertain my

daydream. I decided that he must really be a great . . . person? That just made me wonder what the heck he was, again.

When I'd run past my mother on the way out of the house, she hadn't seemed to notice him at all.

Then when I was running through town, talking to him the whole time, no one in the street had so much as cast a glance in his direction. I guess everyone was just too focused on me.

Could it be that I looked THAT good in my new uniform!? I could only wish. Upon further inspection it was clear that no one was looking at me that way.

In fact, it kind of looked like they were thinking, "What's wrong with that girl?" or "Why does she keep talking to herself?"

While I was thinking it over, Bimii cleared his throat loudly and answered my question for me. "I forgot to mention this during your interview. Only those students who have been accepted to our academy can see me, ryui. Only the chosen people can hear what I say, ryui!"

"Might you happen to mean Chuunibyou syndrome*?"

I looked at Bimii a little more carefully than I had before.

He'd said "chosen people," which had a really dramatic ring to it.

"That's not it at all, ryui! And why are you so polite all of a sudden? Are you trying to distance yourself from me, ryui!?"

"Sorry! What were you saying about the seal on your left hand? It hurts or something?"

"I didn't say anything like that! Stop acting like you think you're so funny, ryui!"

If Bimii was telling the truth, to all the people around me, it would look like I was getting in a shouting match with myself. It suddenly hit home how crazy I must have looked. I felt a cold breeze blow over me.

Thinking of the pointless conversations we just had, I must have seemed crazy.

"I have a few questions for you, ryui. It's nothing important. I hope you'll entertain me, ryui. Okay, question number one! What is your favorite animal?"

"I like gorillas!"

"Gorillas? I didn't expect you to say that, ryui! Okay, next question. Do you want to get married when you grow up?"

"Yes! I want to be a bride!"

"I guess that makes you a pretty average girl, ryui. Next! I heard that you were pretty impressed with the girl who modeled the school uniforms. What about her appealed to you?"

"She was really cool. I really want to be held against her chest!"

"You look so serious. It's a little intimidating, ryui! Oh, here's another one. What do you like to do for exercise?

"I like dancing! Do you want to see me dance?"

"We're in a hurry right now, but maybe you could show me later, ryui. Sorry to keep changing the subject, but what sound does a gorilla make? I've completely forgotten, ryui."

"U-ho-ho! U-ho-ho!" I tried to make it easier for him to picture by swinging my arms and swaying from side to side. I can be very considerate when I set my mind to it.

"Thank you! Oh hey, ryui! We're almost at the station, ryui!"

Yeah, that's how it went. Of course, at the time I

didn't know that the people around me weren't able to see Bimii. So to the bombshell mother and her beautiful baby standing nearby, it must have looked like I was talking to myself.

Picturing it from their perspective, it must have gone like this:

"I like gorillas (my eyes sparkling)! I want to be a bride (looking off wistfully)! I really want to be held against that chest! (Then like I remembered something) I like dancing! Wanna see me dance? (Beating my chest and swaying.) U-ho-ho! U-ho-ho!"

Ahhhhhhhh! Oh no!

I couldn't believe it! Have you ever heard of such a tragedy?

Had I just blurted out to the city, red-faced, that I wanted to marry a gorilla? And did I follow that exclamation up with a gorilla dance, all by myself?

I'd thrown myself into it, too, swinging my arms and my legs in a—pretty good—gorilla impression. Oh no . . . I wanted to die. I really did.

That pretty mother and her beautiful baby must have been terrified.

"Mommy? What's that girl doing? Is she a gorilla?"

"Shh! Don't look at her! Don't look her in the eyes! It's almost summer. All the weirdos are starting to come out. We better be careful!"

"Okay!"

If that was the conversation they'd had about me then I suppose I couldn't blame them.

I could picture it all as clear as day. The balding principal at the local elementary school would have mentioned the event in his morning assembly address.

"There have been reports in the area of a strange person who seems to believe she is a gorilla. Do not walk to school unattended until we can verify these reports!"

Or what if it evolved into an urban legend, spread among the town children? They'd call me the "gorilla woman" and their parents would say things like, "If you aren't a good boy, the gorilla woman will come and dance you to death!" And the kids would scream in terror and apologize for whatever they'd done to make their parents mad. Yes, I could picture it all, clear as day.

And that's not to mention what they'd say of me on the Internet. The denizens of the Internet would turn me into a meme. Pretty soon there would be drawings and pictures of the gorilla woman everywhere. They'd make images of me when requested, like "I need a picture of the gorilla woman carrying a fire hose to a burning building!"

I'd be everyone's little plaything.

My imagination wouldn't let me stop picturing the possibilities. It was getting out of hand. I didn't know how to stop it. I broke out in a cold sweat.

"Eruna, what's wrong, ryui?"

That was Bimii. His deep masculine voice was just as mismatched to his cute body and catchphrase as it ever was, but for some reason the look of him bothered me tremendously.

I shot him the nastiest look I could manage. He looked startled and shouted, "Ryui? Ah! Are you doing the gorilla impression again? Impressive! You really capture that wild, primitive need for violence, ryui!"

He clapped with joy while he appraised my "impersonation" skills.

Dear teacher, is it wrong for me to punish this flying creature? I think he needs to be punished, at least a little. The little monster!

If I attacked Bimii, I'd just look crazy to the people around me. They'd think I was a gorilla on the rampage! Right—I couldn't afford to open myself up to more rumormongering . . . or could I? I couldn't hold myself back any longer.

I readied my feet and dashed at the little beast. Clutching my hands together as if I were holding a bat, I swung my arms as hard as I could at him.

"Bimiiiiiii!" My face was as red as a tomato, and my voice was so shrill it broke. I was sure that no one could have understood what I was saying with my voice like that. I sounded like a demon crawling to the surface world from the depths of hell. But my fists met their target with a crash, and Bimii went flying.

I could only assume how my latest action would affect the tales of the gorilla woman. Would everyone start saying that the gorilla woman shouts "Bimii!" before she attacks? Would they think it was my catchphrase?

"What . . . What was that for, ryui!?"

Bimii called out to me from high in the air, where my attack had sent him tumbling. Unable to understand what had just happened, he floated there confused, a question mark blinking over his head.

We hadn't yet had the opportunity to really get to know each other, so the awkwardness that resulted from my attack took a long time to go away.

"Rumph!" Bimii puffed out his cheeks and turned his back to me. I could only assume that "rumph" was his attempt at a human "hmph!"

This little beast was kind of hard to understand.

I really wanted to tell him that he didn't need to incorporate his catchphrase into everything he said. But it sort of felt like we were in the middle of a whoever-speaks-first-loses contest. So I didn't say anything.

I'd manage to waste plenty of time with my antics, but I still didn't know how to get to the school.

I was standing there, mouth agape, trying to figure out what to do, when a fancy car drove up and coasted to a silent stop right in front of me. It was the sort of fancy car that broadcasted, "Only millionaires allowed. Gorilla women may be permitted to ride in the trunk."

I still hadn't gotten over my sense of victimization (really just the result of my own delusional imagination) when the door slowly swung open and out stepped . . .

"Kurumi-san!?"

The person that stepped from the driver's seat was

none other than the maid I'd met at the test site, Kurumi-san. That's right, I'd named her that because she was like a cool, beautiful mirage. On second thought, maybe I'd rushed too much to come up with a nickname for her.

Seeing her out in the normal town in her maid outfit struck me as an extremely bizarre sight. But then I caught sight of Bimii flapping down to meet her and I realized I had no idea what "normal" really meant.

Up until that day, I'd been leading a normal, healthy, sincere life (I'm sure that my family and friends would have something to say about that), but all of a sudden everything was topsy-turvy!

"Eruna, this car will take us to the academy, ryui! Let's get in, ryuiiii!"

Bimii had taken the high route by addressing me. He seemed to be secretly implying that he was the real adult and that he wouldn't waste time needlessly extending a fight. Feeling a little bit like I'd lost our battle of wits, I climbed into the back seat of the car.

Kurumi-san hadn't really come to pick me up on purpose. Damn! Having a maid or a butler was always a dream of mine.

"What is with this seat? It's so soft! It feels so good on my butt! Is it made for royalty? Is it made for royalty with hemorrhoids?"

"I don't think so, ryui!"

Bimii looked at me disappointedly while I bounced up and down on the seat. I wished he wouldn't look at me with all that pity in his eyes.

I couldn't wrap my mind around why they would make a seat this comfortable if it wasn't for some kind of royalty. I set my chin on my fist and thought seriously about it, but the car started rolling away before I could come up with an answer.

"Oh, don't forget to buckle up for safety!" Bimii said.

I took a look at the seatbelt. It was clearly too large to do me any good. I pretended not to hear him protesting beside me.

Outside the window, the town I'd lived in since I was born rolled by.

"As you know, the private Mikagura Academy houses its students on campus. Except for dire circumstances, students are generally not permitted to return to their homes, ryui."

I assumed he was trying to tell me that I better take one last long look at my hometown.

I'm not normally the type to lapse into sentimentality. I felt a little wistful as I watched my town grow smaller in the rearview mirror. Each time we passed a place where I'd made memories, I felt a twinge of nostalgia. To anyone else, those places wouldn't have seemed special in any way. For me, because of my memories, they sparkled with significance. I wouldn't—couldn't—forget them.

We passed a park that I used to play in with Shigure (though at the time, of course, I'd considered it a favor to him). I don't know what had happened, but all the playground equipment was gone, and there were tall weeds growing in patches all over it. There wasn't a single kid playing there.

I could remember how it had been in the past if I just closed my eyes. I used to play in the park, and my favorite game was one I'd invented. I called it "Perverts!"

I used to pretend that I was a pervert and creep around the playground saying things like, "Eh heh heh . . . Hey there little girl! Want to go to a neat place with me?" It was mostly just tag, but the pervert was "it." I had to run around slowly and make sure I didn't catch anyone.

I came up with that last rule because perverts are obviously slow runners (that's how I pictured them when I was a kid).

Any kid that didn't really get into the role would be left out of the game. So everyone really tried their best. In hindsight, it was a pretty adult game.

If you were caught, you became a pervert, too. The longer the game went on the more perverts there were on the playground. By the time the sun started going down, the playground was almost entirely full of perverts. Kids that weren't used to the game used to get so upset they would cry and run away. It must have looked like an eerie, mysterious scene to any adults that were watching. Some game, right?

Shigure was the best. He was the most convincing pervert I'd ever seen. Very charismatic. It was like he was destined to become a world-class pervert when he grew up.

Shortly after those pervert game days, we had a meeting at school and they told us that we couldn't play at that park anymore. I guess it has been empty since then.

"Ryui!? Isn't that all your fault, ryui!?"

"How dare you say such a thing!"

I hadn't expected to get reprimanded! I was right in the middle of getting sentimental! Jeez, he had to ruin it.

Adults had always been mad at me for it. I developed a reputation as a *troubled* kid. But I'd also managed to make a lot of friends there. In the end, I think it was all just innocent fun.

I wasn't a child anymore and of course I didn't do such foolish things. But looking back on it all, I think I'd made the most of my time there. I'd done my best to make each day exciting.

Right. That's what I wanted. I reconfirmed my ambitions just in time to see the car pull into the academy. I must have been lost in thought for a while, because we were way out in the mountains and completely surrounded by untouched nature. The campus was surrounded by wilderness. I rolled down the window and leaned out to breathe in the mountain air. "Wow! Is this really it?" I exclaimed. My scarf and hair trailed behind me on the breeze.

Bimii slipped out from under his seatbelt and flew alongside the car as he explained, "Welcome to

Mikagura Academy! As the instructor representative, allow me to welcome you to our institution, ryui!"

"Thank you. Wait, instructor!?"

That was an unexpected piece of information. An announcement you just can't ignore!

"Shut up," I whispered, quietly enough that Kurumi-san wouldn't be able to hear me. There we were, a rambunctious girl-creature duo, pulling through the academy gates, driven by a maid.

There was a light chime ringing off in the distance. I didn't realize at the time that it was probably signaling the end of the entrance ceremony.

The car passed under a strange archway, formed from the intertwined branches of trees, and finally we caught site of the main school building.

It was so large and opulent that I could hardly take it all in.

*

"It wasn't supposed to be like this!"

Alright, back to how this all started. No matter how many times I screamed, it never felt like enough. The ceremony had been over for a while by the time I got there. But I guess I can admit fault for that, since I slept so late that day. And sure, I had to join the welcome party—I had really been looking forward to it—halfway through. That was my fault, too. You reap what you sow, as they say.

Having waited, and waited, for my late arrival, my cousin Shigure came running over to me and offered some consolation.

"It's okay. I'm sure you're a little surprised. It will take a little getting used to. Once you're accustomed to it, you'll see that this is the best school ever!" He sounded very proud of the place, and he tried to calm me down by flashing a shy smile, the same one he'd had since childhood.

Girls off in the distance were shouting in excited, ear-splitting, shrill voices.

There were a lot of girls at the school who couldn't get enough of his looks and that vibe he always tried (though I never fell for) to impress on me—the dependable older brother kind of vibe.

I couldn't understand how girls could always prop up his absurd self-image. I certainly wasn't going to fall for it. I pouted to show how unimpressed I was, hoping he'd hurry the conversation along.

"One of the most interesting things about the academy is that every student must join a club of some kind."

"Yes, and only culture-themed clubs are allowed here, ryui!" Bimii chirped from his perch on my shoulder.

"Oh yeah, I think the pamphlet said something about that."

When I'd flipped through it, my attention had been captured by the cute uniforms, not to mention that bodacious model. I hadn't really paid much attention to anything else.

Of course, I'd noticed that the academy students were obligated to stay in the school dorms, but the rest of the pamphlet had looked like every other school out there. Or at least, that's what I'd thought. Granted, it was rare for a school to not offer any sports clubs. I hadn't thought that was interesting enough to warrant much shock or attention.

As for myself, I'd always skewed towards the sports end of the spectrum. I had a knack for sports, to the extent that team captains competed to get me to join. My report cards had often included handwritten rejoinders lamenting the fact that my aptitude for sports hadn't translated in to aptitude for studies. Needless to say, a lack of sports wasn't a very good thing for someone like me.

"And just so you know, they went over most of this stuff during the entrance ceremony."

"Yes, ryui! New students have one month to decide which club they want to join, ryui. If you cannot make up your mind by then, you will be expelled from the academy. Make sure that doesn't happen to you, ryui!"

Well, well! I'm glad someone finally mentioned that! If no one had told me, I'd have ended up in trouble for sure. "Expelled!? Isn't that a little extreme? Why do they have to be so strict? Ugh! I don't know if I can handle it! The rules and regulations are strangling me! I can't breathe!" I shouted, pretending to choke.

I had never heard of anyone getting expelled over something so trivial.

After all I'd been through! After finally earning admission to an academy of real merit! After finally accepting the mantle of the coveted high-school-girl brand! I could hardly bear the thought of losing all that.

I'd always thought that high school girls could get away with anything they wanted. The world is full of unexpected developments, isn't it? It's like, let's say that you're on a really crowded train and everyone is crammed in super tight. And there is a really pretty office lady, who, if you really want to know, seems like she's really tough, but actually has a soft side that she doesn't show anyone. It's that gap between how she appears and how she is on the inside that gets you all excited. So you "accidentally" bury your face in her boobs (because the train is so crowded) and she screams. But instead of being mad at you, all that she says is, "Oh you're a high school girl! Well, I'm not offended at all! In fact, I love having girls around because I feel like we understand each other. Why don't you squeeze a little closer?" And then she pulls you closer against her for the rest of the commute. I'd always thought that life was like that for high school girls.

Lost in thought for a moment, I suddenly realized a very long strand of very un-high-school-girl-like drool was threatening to escape from my mouth.

Or let's say you learned to play guitar and posted a

video of yourself playing it. Because you had just started learning and had no idea what you were doing, it was really bad. People would just say, "Oh look how hard she's trying!" or "She should put on a shorter skirt!" or "What a pretty smile!" or "What school does she go to? I want to be friends with her!" or "I can't wait for the next video!"

Everyone would have nice things to say that had nothing to do with your guitar skills, just with how much they liked you!

Right, high school girls are supposed to be able to get away with whatever they want, based on their age and gender alone. Right?

Or let's say that you decided to start making videos on the Internet and you put up a video where you basically didn't have anything to say about anything. You just gabbed a little bit about whatever gossip was popular that day (of course the camera would only focus on your face talking for the whole time). People would say things like, "First time viewer, subscribed!" or "How cute! Where do you live? Can we hang out?" or "Clap, clap, clap," or "How fashionable! Stand up and let us see your whole outfit! Make sure the camera stays focused, and let us see everything!"

Right, if you were a high school girl, then people would love you even if you were an idiot. They would love you *because* you were an idiot.

If you didn't have the high-school-girl brand on your side, or especially if you were a high school boy, then you'd just end up with no views and no comments, and you'd just have to mutter your sad words into the microphone by yourself before crying yourself to sleep.

Thinking it through, I realized that I absolutely had to keep myself enrolled in the academy.

"Eruna, I think you might be a little biased, ryui," Bimii sighed, exhausted from dealing with me. But I think I had made my point—I really didn't want to be expelled. Maybe I'd gotten a little carried away.

Regardless, the scene that was unfolding before my eyes, these student clubs and their performances, were completely unbelievable. I almost suspected that I was being pranked, that this was all some sort of hidden camera TV show set up.

It was so shocking that I felt dizzy.

Thinking the other new students must have felt as overwhelmed as I did, I looked around to see how others were reacting. It was clear that I was the only one surprised by what was going on. Almost everyone looked thrilled by it. Their eyes were wide and sparkling and full of adoration. Was I the weird one here? ME!?

It was basically a normal, peaceful party. But then the peace was broken by an aggressive, violent scream.

"Why are you making that face? Why are you acting like you're going to cry? You're making it look like I'm the bad guy here!"

"I'm sorry! I'm sorry! I didn't mean to!"

A blond boy with a ragged-looking uniform was shouting at a new student that was collapsed on the ground before him. It seems that the boy had been knocked over just by brushing against the blond boy and that had pissed the blond boy off. It probably wasn't actually a very big deal. There was no denying that they were throwing water on the happy mood the party had up until then.

"That's the Art Club representative, Kuzuryu-kun. He was on stage just a second ago. As for the kid on the ground, I feel like I've seen him somewhere before, but I guess he's new." Shigure noticed that I was watching them closely, and he leaned over to fill me in.

I knew what an Art Club was, but what did it mean to be its "representative?"

Whatever, that didn't matter. What I was witnessing wasn't *right*. Ever since I was little, I had a strangely strong sense of justice. I could never just stand back and watch a fight. Sure, that tendency had gotten me in trouble before, but I wasn't the sort of girl who could just look the other way.

I took a breath, puffed my chest out, and walked toward them. Shigure reached out to stop me, as if I were a baby, so I slapped his hand away and moved on.

"Ha! Look what you've gotten yourself into. Now everyone is watching. Is that what you wanted? Is that why you did this? You girly little rookie!"

"You're wrong! I just . . . I just want to apologize for bumping into you! But . . ."

No one else looked like they wanted to butt into the uncomfortable situation. Everyone was standing back and letting it get worse and worse.

I looked around for teachers, but I didn't see any around. Bimii was just watching them as if he found it entertaining. From where I stood, all I could see was an upperclassman picking on a poor new student! I couldn't allow it to continue!

I threw my arms open wide and skipped over to stand between the two of them.

"That's enough! Stop! Stop!" Aaaaaaand . . . Step! Step!

I lightly clicked my heels and tried to arbitrate their disagreement. Everyone said that my lack of consideration, of tension, was my worst (and best) character trait.

I wasn't sure if I had managed a skillful negotiation or not. The two of them stopped fighting for a second and stared at me in silence. I suddenly realized that it wasn't that they were thrilled a mediator had stepped in, but more that they were baffled by what I was doing there. The whole time, I kept up my little dance. I started to really get into it.

"Hm! Hey! Hey! Hoy! Hm!" Now the whole area was silent. My rhythmic shouts echoed over the crowd. I caught sight of Shigure covering his eyes and pretending he didn't know me. He slowly backed away to put the crowd between us. I couldn't blame him for that. I was starting to wonder what the heck I was doing, too!

The crowd started to murmur and the murmuring had the distinct tone of "what is with the new girl?" Kuzuryu, the leader of the Art Club, turned to me with a look of exhaustion.

"What do you want? Did you have something to say?"

He spoke in a controlled tone. I could tell that he was very annoyed.

He was scary, but I wasn't about to back down!

Not only did I have a strong sense of justice, but I was really good at sports, too. And I was a maiden—no, an ANGEL! (Was I getting ahead of myself?)

I tensed up, afraid that he might hit me.

I finally stopped dancing. I stood there in silence as Kuzuryu stepped up to me. Just when he was about to speak . . .

"That's about enough of that," a kind voice, full of integrity, interjected. And the air quivered.

I turned to see who had spoken and saw a goddess.

That's not an exaggeration either. It was *her*, the girl of my dreams, the girl that had convinced me to apply to the academy in the first place.

She was dainty and perfectly composed, poetically beautiful. She was really the most beautiful person that I had ever seen. Her long black hair was shiny and flowed like water over her shoulders. It was the sort of hair that looked like it should be illegal. It was too perfect! She flipped it and I imagined it wafting a lovely smell in my direction.

She was so stunning I couldn't think of anything to say. I might have been imagining it, but I think that when she saw me standing there in silence she smiled at me, just a little.

"Kuzuryu-san, is this really worth getting so worked up over? These are our adorable new classmates, after all. We should be looking out for them."

She'd modeled the uniform in the school pamphlet, but from the picture I could never have guessed how beautiful her voice was! How could one girl be so blessed?

She didn't speak from a high horse either. She spoke as if we were equals. She was so composed and kind that you'd have second thoughts if you had to disagree with her. In comparison, my attempt at mediation looked ridiculous. What was I thinking? Step! Dance! You *idiot*, you got carried away again! Aren't you ashamed? Aren't you?

Without realizing it, I had started to berate myself silently.

"Worked up? Ha! You must be joking. I was just looking out for the guy."

Kuzuryu barked, looking very annoyed. Then he shrugged as if he'd lost interest and walked away.

Everyone must have been afraid of him, because the crowd split to let him pass and closed again after he'd left.

Sighing as if she'd resigned herself to the situation, the goddess walked over and helped the boy to his feet.

The boy looked as if he was having trouble processing all that had happened. His eyes went wide and he bowed deeply, a few times in a row, shouting, "Thank you! Thank you so much!"

"I know that Kuzuryu-san looks like a scary person, but the truth is that he's not that bad. Don't worry about it, okay?"

Whoaaaaaa.

I couldn't help but to get excited over her. It was HER. The goddess from the pamphlet! It was really her! The girl that I wanted to marry! (According to my own research, everyone wanted to marry her.) No retouching, no Photoshop, no adjustments—just 100 percent real beauty!

It was the sort of beauty that was so stunning I needed a pinch on the cheek. I ran over to Shigure and slapped him hard, but I didn't wake from my dream. (Why did I do that?) I stood there sputtering like a baby and opening and closing my eyes to see if she would disappear. But she was there the whole time.

I wanted to be just like her! The perfect model of all my teenage fantasies had finally appeared to save me! She's arrived to show me that I couldn't even imagine, couldn't even hallucinate, anything better in the world.

I hadn't said a word yet. My infatuation was clear from the look on my face, because she turned in my direction and said, "Hm?"

I was panting like a dog, my tongue lolling from my mouth, and staring at her with laser-like focus. I suppose it was only natural that she was confused. Oh well, so much for my plan for an elegant high school debut. I just couldn't control myself!

"I see. So you're after her now?"

Who was the goddess talking to?

I followed her gaze to find her looking at Bimii, who was flying around with a serious look on his face.

Did those two know each other? Whoops! Sorry,

Bimii! I hoped he'd forgive me for all I'd done up until then. I'm sorry for everything! I apologize for everything since naming him "Bimii." I'd apologize for whatever he wanted, anything, if only he would introduce me to her! I'd get down on my knees and beg if I had to! Just please, please introduce me!

Clap, clap!

That was the sound of the obvious winking I did at Bimii, hoping he'd understand what I meant. He just ignored me.

"I don't know yet either way, ryui. But . . ."

"But?"

I tried desperately to get them to involve me, but they were in their own world and paid me no attention at all.

"Seisa. This girl might have different possibilities than you do, ryui."

"Perhaps."

I had no idea what they were talking about. And it really wasn't the time or place to find out. I had just met the most important person of my life! This would be a pivotal scene in any book that people write about me in the future. A real turning point. A formative experience.

Standing there trying to get their attention, I felt like I might explode. I couldn't stop wondering what they were talking about or when Bimii was going to introduce me.

And then, as if nothing had happened at all, she simply turned and walked away. When I realized she'd left and I hadn't managed to meet her, I wrapped my hands around Shigure's neck and shouted, "What am I going to DO!? WHAT SHOULD I DO? Am I weird? How was my hair? Did I sound weird? Look weird? That was the most important meeting of my life! Did I screw it up? Did I?"

"I . . . I can't breathe . . . I want you to love me, but not like this! Be normal!"

That was all after he'd told me that my normal personality was weird and that I had too many other things to worry about before I should even think about my hair. I was so shocked I couldn't believe what I was hearing.

"Oh no."

Even though I'm a pure Japanese, I'd been so thrown off that I'd been ridiculous and reacted like a foreigner.

It was fine. It looked like she'd noticed me and talked about me with Bimii, which was about as much as I could hope for on my first day. I needed to stay positive! *Let's positive thinking! Yay!*

. . . There I went again, freaking out like a flamboyant foreigner. I guess I hadn't quite come to my senses.

Even though I was standing there looking insane, the poor boy who'd gotten caught up in all the trouble with Kuzuryu came over and bowed to me.

"Um . . . Thank you very much! I'm a new first-year student. My name is Asuhi Imizu. I went to Mikagura Middle School, too."

He had blue hair and looked very delicate. His voice was high, and he sounded frail. I wouldn't have been surprised if he confessed to actually being a girl. There was something distinctly feminine about him.

He was kind of funny, I guess, but there was nothing wrong with him that I could tell.

"Oh, it was nothing. I tried to help but just ended up doing a stupid dance! All I ended up doing was making a fool out of myself. Oh, I'm Eruna Ichinomiya. I'm a first-year student, too! Nice to meet you!"

I laughed and held out my hand to him. He was very

skittish. It took him a while to decide if he was going to shake it or not. Holding out his hand, then getting scared, eventually he shook my hand. His hand was so small and thin! And his skin was so smooth! Was he really a girl? He looked like he'd stepped right out of a dating simulator for girls! Was he waiting for me to go on the offensive? Was that it?

I wanted to yell at him for being so darn cute! But of course I didn't say that. I just shook his hand nice and hard and that was it.

". . . ? Nice to meet you."

He looked confused and a little scared, but that's just the way I like them!

Fine, good! I approved!

He was holding something that had been bothering me that whole time. I couldn't keep myself from asking about it any longer.

"Hey, Asuhi? What's that?"

I had to know. He was so small that the massive thing he was holding wasn't suited to his body size at all. In fact, the reason he'd bumped into Kuzuryu was because the large object had thrown him off balance.

"This is a telescope for astronomy. I've been in astronomy clubs for years!"

"Ooooh, a telescope. Neat! I approve! That's a really big one!"

I nodded and looked the thing over. All I did was look at his telescope, but for some reason Asuhi got very embarrassed and his face flushed bright red.

Astronomy, hm . . . I guess he was planning on joining an astronomy club again now that he was in high school.

I was only good at sports. I had no idea what club I was suited for at Mikagura. I sort of thought that maybe I wasn't suited for any of them.

"The school is pretty far from town, so there's not much light to interfere with stargazing. The view from the roof is remarkably clear! If you're interested Ichinomiya-san . . . I mean, Eruna . . . Please stop by some time."

This kid was so cuuute! I loved it when boys spoke up to me that way. And when he talked about the stars, he spoke a little quicker, a little more confidently. How cute! I wished I could lean over and nibble on his little cheeks. And did you notice that he called me by my last name and then dug down for courage to call me by my first name? Cuuuute. So cute.

I had to respond in a way that wouldn't scare him off. I had to show him how cool and collected I was.

"Definitely, I'd love to watch the stars someday."

"Great! See you then! Oh, one more thing!"

"What's that?"

He ran over to Shigure and excitedly exclaimed, "You're Shigure Ninomiya, the representative of the Manga Research Club, aren't you? I've wanted to join for years! I, um . . . um . . . I just wanted to tell you that!"

Asuhi bowed politely and left with some hesitation. He was a cute little boy from the second I saw him until the second he left. Damn.

What was up with the way he left? Did I just have a dirty mind? I couldn't help but imagine him as the protagonist of a boy's love manga—how exciting! Was I overthinking it?

Personally, I wasn't particularly interested in the genre, but I had friends that were, so I knew a little bit about it.

"Hey Shigure, you're the 'representative' of the Manga Research Club, right? I wondered about this when I met Kuzuryu. What is the difference between the club president and its representative?"

"I'm the president AND the representative. But I guess I shouldn't expect you to know all about that yet, right, Eruna? Should I explain Mikagura's unique club battle system?"

"Club battle?"

I'd never heard of anything like that. I imagined that it was something akin to a field day?

How could they have a field day if the academy only permitted culture-themed clubs?

The more I thought about it, the more confused I got, so I gave up thinking altogether and just asked him to explain.

"How about you let a real instructor explain, ryui? Here at Mikagura Academy, our clubs periodically compete with each other through our special battle system. The clubs are all ranked against each other based on the outcome of these battles, ryui."

"Battles? How are culture clubs supposed to decided who wins these competitions? I don't get it."

It was a stupid question. The events occurring during the 'party' around me had made the answer perfectly clear. Just thinking about it made my head hurt. What had I gotten myself into with this place?

I felt like I didn't even understand what a culture-themed school club WAS anymore. The different clubs seemed to have items that were vaguely related to the subject matter of the club, but they were attacking one another with those items. Some of them were doing really crazy things like shooting laser beams, making giant flowers that exploded like natural disasters, and filling the whole area with sparkling, flashing lights. I couldn't make heads or tails of any of it. So much of what I was seeing was nonsensical. And even though I was blessed with an innate ability to bestow names on things or people, I was at a loss.

Bimii didn't seem to realize how confused I was, as he just went on explaining.

"The club representatives are individuals that are chosen by the members of each club to represent the club in battle, ryui. You see how that's different from the club president, ryui?"

"Exactly! So I bet you see why it's so impressive that I'm BOTH the president and the representative, right? If you want to fall in love with me, go right ahead."

". . ."

"If you want to fall in love with me, go right ahead!"

I'd purposefully ignored him because he disgusted me. He must have thought I couldn't hear him, because he repeated himself, louder. What was I supposed to do? Could I have him arrested? I'd have to get in touch with a judge.

It struck me that, because the students lived in dorms on campus, I'd have to look at his stupid face all the time. The very thought wore me out. He clearly didn't understand how I felt, because he started to wink at me. So I imagined spraying him in the face with a bottle of pesticide. That calmed me down a bit.

"There are different kinds of battles. The most special and influential are the midterm qualifiers and the final battles, ryui. Aside from those, there are academy-arranged single battles, and for the first-year students, rookie battles, ryui. The outcomes of these battles have a heavy influence on the way that dorm rooms are assigned, where and what the students eat, and on all aspects of student life at the academy, ryui."

"If you're a member of a high-ranking club, then you get to live in the biggest dorm rooms with the nicest furniture. Your meals are more luxurious and fancy!"

Now that sounded pretty interesting—at least the

parts I had understood did. I tried to process all the new information, but the two of them kept talking without pause.

"Wow! Well, I can't really keep up with everything you're saying. It sure sounds impressive! I feel like I'm at a festival or something! It sounds fun!"

There was more to school than studying. The academy was stimulating and exciting to the point where I wondered if they had banned any use of the word "boring."

But why hadn't they included any of this information in the pamphlet? At the very least, you'd think they could have mentioned it at the test site or during the interview! Still, even if they had told me all about this weird place, I think I might have chosen to apply anyway.

I was up for it! This place was a fantasy. It was like a dream! I had no desire to hide my excitement and surprise. Half of me wanted to nod along, as if this were the most normal thing in the world. The other half was freaking out. The first half was stronger though. It was only a matter of time before it did away with my hesitant side. I was just fine with that.

From all the things I'd heard, it sounded like the club you decided to join would have a big impact on your life. It would even determine your room and what you are.

Noticing that I was thinking about it, Bimii chirped, "There are clubs that aren't part of this welcome party, so this isn't all of them. I'll introduce you to all the club representatives that are here, ryui!" He could be a considerate . . . thing . . . when he wanted to.

"Yes! Please! Can you start with that one? I've been wondering about that giant brush she's using since I got here. Can she handle herself okay? She looks small."

It was a young girl with black hair and large eyes. She wore a hakama*. Her eyes were large and alert. She was swinging a gigantic brush at her opponent. With each thrust she shouted, "Hya! Unya! If you please!"

Her little exclamations were cute, especially that "if you please!" I wasn't sure if it made for a good attack shout though. Still, seeing her so invested in battle made you want to run over and give her a big hug. My closest friends (like Shigure or . . . Shigure) were probably obsessed with her.

"She's the representative of the Calligraphy Club,

Himi Yasaka. She might look small, but she's only a second year. She's already at the top of the club. She's an amazing student, ryui!"

"Ah, heh, heh. I can't get enough of this. DID YOU SAY SECOND YEAR!? But she's so small!"

I'd assumed she was a first-year student, like me. To be honest, I could have mistaken her for a middle school student. Still, her footing was elegant and studied. The way she commanded the giant brush made it clear that she could exercise some serious power. The representatives must be pretty impressive people. Still, as far as I know, that's not how you're supposed to use a calligraphy brush.

"I get it now! So the Calligraphy Club fights with giant brushes, right? I guess that makes sense."

When they'd told me that the clubs battled each other, I had a hard time picturing what that actually meant. Now it all seemed so simple. I guess I was really starting to keep up with what was going on. Yup, no problem at all! Even if I woke up in an online RPG, I'd have no problem figuring it out.

While I stared at Himi, I daydreamed about myself running through an RPG world in light armor and two swords at my side. (Of course I'd use two swords.)

"Oh man, I can't . . . I . . . I want to kidnap her!"

"You said that out loud, ryui!"

Whoops, I really needed to stop doing that. Considering how cute this girl was, her mother must have been a real babe.

I bet they looked and sounded just like each other. I bet people often confused them for sisters.

"Oh man, I want to kidnap her and demand a ransom and then look at her pretty mom's worried face. I bet she'd have pretty tears in her eyes."

Shigure looked startled beside me.

"Eruna? What are you saying?"

"It's not a crime to just imagine it, is it? I'm the master of my imagination, aren't I? What's wrong with kidnapping a girl or two?"

"Um . . . sure. Right . . ."

He was looking at me like he wanted to take me to a hospital. Even though we'd been close for so long, Shigure still just didn't understand. Dragging me to a hospital when I'm in imagination mode won't do anyone any good at all! I'd just get to the hospital and start imagining that Himi-chan was my nurse. She'd wear a little mini skirt, and I'd be the doctor, and I'd have to scold Himi-chan for some mistake she'd made at work. Yup, once I let my mind start wandering, there was nothing anyone could do to stop me!

"I'll introduce you to the next representative, ryui."

"Just a second. This part's important. I was just about to start an ear examination."

"So you're already at the hospital in your story? Ryui! And this is after you kidnapped someone?"

Himi-chan sure was cute when she was embarrassed. *It won't hurt or anything, I'm just checking to make sure that you're healthy! If you close your eyes it will all be over in a second.*

My arms were bigger than I'd thought they'd be. I reached them out slowly. I was so close! I was almost to the base of the soft, soft mountain . . . But then—

"Aahhh! Let's move on to the Drama Club, ryui! The representative is a second-year student names Yuto Akama. He's a pretty accomplished actor. You can't argue with that, ryui!"

Bimii was shouting loud enough to drown out my overactive imagination. How rude! I was at the best part! I'd have to save my Himi mountain climbing for another day.

"Drama Club!? It looks like he's fighting with a giant scythe, like the angel of death or something. How cool! I want to try swinging it, too!"

The effect was one of overstated importance and a concern for aesthetics—I loved it! I wanted to hold it and say something like, "The meteor shower will be celebrated on the anniversary of your death!" I'd squint my eyes when I said it, and I wouldn't smile at all.

The person I was talking to would say, "When is the meteor shower? Am I safe if there's only one shooting star? If there's only one, can I wish on it? And by the way, what do you mean the anniversary of my death? I don't really get it." That would be great.

Calm down, Eruna. Focus.

The second thing I noticed about him was his leopard hat, which was colorful and patterned and even had ears. It made him look fun, likable, and a little mysterious.

His bangs were long and covered his left eye. The exposed right eye was scanning the crowd looking for new students to challenge.

"Wow, there are so many interesting new people! Interesting for sure, but none of them look like they could match my ability on stage! Ha!"

"Akama thinks of everything in terms of drama. Maybe we should make the protagonist of the next production a girl, hm? Then he wouldn't be able to make himself the star."

"I think I could pull off a girl character just fine. If I had a good costume, I'd be better than a real one!"

"Better than a real one? Give me a break! You're going to have to give up the spotlight some day!"

Friends from the Drama Club had formed a circle around him. They were all talking jovially. The boys and girls were all dressed in animal-patterned clothes. They didn't seem to mind how people looked at them.

I assumed they were all part of the Drama Club. Each one of them was so individualistic! I was looking at them when Shigure leaned over to explain.

"Everyone in the Drama Club gets to play a part no matter what. They dress like that to get into their roles."

"So that's why they're dressed like that. I guess some of them look like dogs or cows. If you were in the Drama Club, I bet you'd be a perverted kappa*."

"There's no such thing! I could make a concession, I suppose, and have you get rid of the pervert part. But I still feel like being a kappa is an insult!"

I stuck up my thumb to show that everything was all good and said, "Make sure you find a good plate for your head!"

"I won't need one!"

I'd only been trying to help, but he insisted on fighting me each step of the way. Oh well.

I don't see what he was so upset about. Kappa weren't so bad, were they? I guess I didn't know.

I still think he could pull it off the kappa role—I mean . . . no wait, *perverted* kappa. He was glaring at me angrily. I pretended not to notice.

"Anyway, the representative of the Drama Club, this Yuto Akama-kun guy, I feel like he's been staring at me this whole time. Do you think it's love at first sight? Do you think he'll be chasing after me forever? That would put me in a tough spot, considering I'm betrothed to the goddess!"

"I think you're imagining things, ryui."

"It's all in your head," said Shigure.

Okay fine.

I didn't like that they both felt the need to chime in, but whatever.

—*Idiot*—

I thought I saw Akama-kun's lips mouth the word. Had I imagined that, too?

"Moving on. That's Sadamatsu Minatogawa, the representative of the Flower Arranging Club. If he looks a little hard to pin down, that's because he is, ryui!"

"What's that supposed to mean? Flower arranging, hm . . . I don't think I'd fit in very well with that crowd."

When I was in elementary school, I used to look at the flowers growing on the side of the road and classify them into either the pretty-flower category or the not-so-much category. But the truth is, I made that distinction based only on whether or not I could eat them. To this day, I only thought of flowers as emergency food.

Actually, thinking back on those days, I think that might have been the reason I had stomach aches so often. I used to insist on eating them with everyone I knew. "These flowers are the best. They're delicious! They're the kind of food you only get to eat after your dad's payday! I'll treat you, so come eat some with me!" In the end, no one ever took me up on my offer. I'd been so serious, so condescending, when I told people that I'd treat them to the flowers. I wonder what they'd thought of me. Had I been the most pretentious girl in the neighborhood?

So anyway, I didn't see myself joining the Flower Arranging Club any time soon.

"Look! Minatogawa-kun can control flowers and plants, ryui!"

"Wow!"

His face was expressionless when he reached his hand out to an empty area and suddenly filled it—seemingly from nothing—with grass. Flowers blossomed. Their petals fluttered on the wind. I wasn't sure how useful a skill like that would be in a battle, but it was definitely pretty to look at.

"Hm."

Just as I was about to nod my approval of his skills, he made a giant flower appear and sat on it with a heavy *thud*.

"What? He only made that thing to sit on it? Is that all that plants are good for?"

For whatever reason, I felt like he'd betrayed my expectations. I'd always believed that plants and flowers deserved our respect (even though I used to pull them out by the roots and eat them!). Jeez! Live and let live!

"He's a little strange, but he's a good guy, ryui."

Apparently not content to use his flower as only

a couch, Minatogawa-kun yawned and looked like he was about to lie down for a nap. I had my doubts about letting someone like him be a club representative, but I guess if he could win battles for his club, then that was all that mattered.

Unlike the Drama Club, I didn't see any other members of the Flower Arranging Club around. He was surrounded by flowers, but he looked all alone. It was a little sad.

"Poor guy . . ." I muttered to myself.

But then, having finished her own battle, the Calligraphy Club's Himi-chan snuck up behind him and shouted, "Boo! Ahaha! Yay! Did I scare you, Minatogawa-kun? Did I startle your socks off?"

Even the way she tried to scare him was cute.

Minatogawa-kun didn't flinch at all. He just cast a peaceful gaze at Himi-chan and said, "Oh yes, you really scared me. My poor heart can't take it."

"That's how you act when you're scared? You're so hard to pin down! If your heart is pounding really hard, you can wait to calm down before you answer me!"

"Can I?"

The two of them looked so peaceful that they were

probably producing negative ions.

They were both dressed in traditional Japanese clothes, too. Maybe they were friends?

"And finally, the one you've been waiting for! Come one, come all! The genius of the school, the super-skilled, the representative of the Manga Research Club, Shigure Ninomiya! His black-framed glasses help him stand out from the crowd. He's Eruna-chan's favorite cousin!" Shigure shouted and struck a pose. No one was listening or looking.

"More like 'tolerated' cousin. Dealing with you takes all the energy I've got. If only there was some way to erase the fact that we are related . . ."

"You mean so that we can get married? I think it's legal for cousins to get married, but I guess you'd rather have a less tainted love affair? Well, I guess I can understand where you're coming from."

His positivity was downright demonic. And the worse part was that I had to admit I shared that personality trait with him! Ugh!

Regardless of how annoying he was, he really was the representative of his club. I could hardly believe that anyone had entrusted him with any responsibility at all. I wanted to yell from the rooftop that they needed a new leader. He was going to sink the ship!

But when I saw the way that the other students were looking at him, I understood Shigure's position.

Their eyes were all dewy with respect and admiration, like little kids looking up to their hero. Please! Everyone! Don't be fooled so easily! You think this guy is your hero? When I was in elementary school he used to come over and help me with my homework. One time I had to write an essay on what I wanted to be when I grew up and he told me that he'd write it for me. When I picked it up the next day it was titled, "When I grow up I want to be Shigure's bride!" Gross, right?

And his handwriting wasn't anything like mine, so the teacher knew I hadn't written it and I got in trouble anyway. I went crying to Shigure. He just laughed at me. Even now, thinking about it makes me angry.

I silently promised myself that I would never join his stupid club.

What was I supposed to do? There were too many to choose from!

"I see that you've already interacted with him. Kyoma Kuzuryu is the representative of the Art Club—

he's a third-year student, ryui! I know that it looks like he likes to pick fights, but he's really not that kind of kid, ryui!"

"Oh yeah? Actually, now that you mention it, he did have paint all over his uniform. Art Club, huh?"

Not to brag, I like to think I can draw pretty well.

I'm the sort of girl who likes to live by her senses, so that probably translated into some level of artistic ability. I even won an art award once (in kindergarten). I was so proud of myself that I never let anyone forget that I'd won, which had really annoyed everyone I knew.

Anyway, if I had to join a club, then the Art Club was probably a decent option.

"Oh, and that kid you just met, the other first-year kid. He was pretty famous back at his middle school. I wouldn't be surprised if he turned out to be the representative of the Astronomy Club," Shigure said, pointing at Asuhi Imizu.

So he was kind of famous? That might explain why Kuzuryu had reacted the way he had.

Mikagura Middle School also used this special club battle system.

If that were true, then kids that had come from

Mikagura Middle School would probably have an advantage over other kids (like me) that had applied from somewhere else. That made me a little worried about my ability to fit in, but I'm sure that everything would be fine. Besides, I wasn't particularly sensitive.

"So what do you think, Eruna? You're going to be living here for the next three years, ryui!"

Of course he felt the need to ask. I had been pretty surprised at first. I even thought that maybe I'd been tricked. I'd felt like killing Shigure.

"I think I'm being punished for my past sins."

"Is it that bad? Are you kind of into it? I guess I can live with that."

Shigure was being a creep again, so I decided to ignore him.

Honestly, after meeting all these people and soaking it all in, my negative first impression had completely vanished.

"I think it's going to be pretty great. It looks fun!" I smiled.

At the very least, it certainly wouldn't be a boring three years. I definitely preferred it to some other school, where every day was the same thing. I could only handle a boring routine for so long.

I might be overstating, but it almost felt like the academy had been built for me specifically—that's how positive I was feeling about it.

I pet Bimii's head (he was sitting on my shoulder) and nodded. Yes, I think I was going to fit in just fine.

The welcome party looked like it was wrapping up. The new students were being given little sheets of paper that included directions to the dorms they'd been assigned to.

"Eruna-chan, you better go get yours, too."

"Whew! I was just starting to think I was going to have to camp out in the woods!"

It would have been fun, curled up under a tree, using Bimii as a pillow. How fun would that have been? Eh?

Shigure passed me a map of the academy campus that indicated the location of the dorms. Considering the fact that all the students were housed on campus, I shouldn't have been surprised to see that there were quite a few dormitories. Had I just wandered around hoping to find the right building, I don't think I ever would have made it.

"And I'll give you this, too. Every student here is given one of these devices because they are not permitted to carry cell phones. This will let you talk to anyone on campus, so you won't miss having a phone."

It looked kind of like a smartphone, but kind of not—I'd never seen anything like it. It seemed to have a lot of different functions, but it also seemed to be simple enough to operate that I could rely on intuition. That was good, because I never liked to read instruction manuals.

It appeared to have campus maps installed on it, so I wouldn't have to spend too much time wandering around lost.

There was one thing that was bothering me about it. "Shigure, why is your contact information already stored in here!? I'm trying to delete it and it's saying that I need a password!"

"I registered myself and locked it—for you, of course. No need to thank me."

It got worse—his contact information was saved under "Nii-chan."

He didn't need to worry about getting any words of gratitude from me!

I had to throw it away. The device was brand new, but it had already been defiled! I had to throw it away!

I set my footing and reared back to put my years of softball training to use. Just as I was about to throw it with all my might . . .

"Oh well."

I decided against it. It would have reflected poorly on me as a new student. I'd have to find some way to carry on.

Shigure smirked, satisfied with his victory. Nothing annoyed me more than that little smirk of his.

"That device is used in all parts of student life here, so make sure that you keep it on you at all times. And don't worry. I'll call every morning to say that I love you!"

"No thank you!"

He wasn't really a bad guy. He knew that I wasn't a morning person. He was probably just trying to help me get adjusted to the new schedule. Why did he have to make it sound so weird and creepy though? Was it because he was secretly shy? Huh, was that it?

Whatever. I realized that I'd have to rely on him in the end.

Still, that sweet, tender, emotional face that he made at me was disgusting. It made me want to throw up. But

I knew that he'd always be there for me, and if anything bad happened, he'd be the first to support me.

"Huh? What's wrong, Eruna-chan?"

"Nothing! I'm going to go check out my room now!"

That was a close one—he almost caught me thinking nice things about him. That would have ruined my day. By the way, I don't know how they did it, but sometime between my application and the welcome party, the administration had figured out what size uniform I needed. Shigure even knew my ring size! *I* didn't even know my ring size! He passed me a notebook that was filled with name ideas for our future children. There were five notebooks, a real mystery. I wanted to rip them up and burn them. The more I thought about it, the more I wondered if we were really related.

Shigure waved to me as I walked away and told me to have fun. I stuck my tongue out at him, and he made a strange face in response. Ha! Whatever!

The other new students had formed a line and filed out of the area, so I ran ahead to join them.

When I left the building, I was greeted by blinding sunlight. I'd learned so much that it felt like I'd been in that building forever, but it was still early enough that the sun hadn't started to go down.

I checked the device to see where the dormitory I'd been assigned to was. I still didn't really have a handle on how large the campus was, so it was hard to tell how far I had to go just by looking at the map.

"Um . . . I guess I'll just start walking?"

"A normal girl could walk to the dorms in ten minutes, ryui! So it should only take you five, ryui!"

"Neat! Then I guess I'll take my time and look around. And hey, I'll have you know that I walk just like everyone else! Why do you think I walk twice as fast as a normal person? What's that supposed to mean?"

Weird creature. But it made me think. How long was Bimii planning on following me around for? Didn't he have anything better to do? He'd said that he was an instructor, didn't he? And just what *was* he anyway? Was he being punished somehow? Was he reincarnated like this because of evil things he'd done in a past life? The gods can be so cruel.

"Um . . . You're talking out loud again, ryui. I can hear you. I wish you'd keep those thoughts eternally private. I can hear them and they sound kind of critical, ryui. And I didn't do anything bad in my past life, ryui."

I guess I'd hurt his feelings. His eyes looked wetter than usual. I guess that meant *I* was the bad guy.

I felt bad about it, so I looked him up and down quickly, trying to find something about him I could compliment.

Everyone has some positive attributes, right? It didn't have to be anything big to be worth pointing out. Something the size of a pinhead would be good enough. Or maybe, I just needed to work on my delivery. Me? Even though everyone knew I was a wizard when it came to words? Granted, no one had ever called me that to my face, but everyone knew that I was the best and that I could do anything! That I had a *dexterous mind*. I like the sound of that: *dexterous mind*. Heh!

"Um . . ."

"It makes me nervous when you stare at me like that, ryui."

He sat there twitching and it made me feel . . . how to put this . . . what was the feeling? Like I wanted to punch him? Like I HAD to punch him? No! I shouldn't. I stopped myself from hitting him. Right. If I was going to say something nice about him, now was the time. I could punch him after that.

Wait, so I could still punch him? Really? Oh right, because of . . .

Wait, because of what?

So I kept looking him over, but I couldn't think of anything nice to say. He just looked like someone had tried to make a cat and failed. And what was with the wings? If they were on anything but Bimii, they might have even been cute! They were so small. I didn't understand how he could fly with such small wings. I had to ask about that later. Or maybe I should ask—no! Demand to know how they worked now. No? Anyway, if I had to compliment him, maybe the wings would be a good place to start.

Yup, that was all I could think of. The pressure was starting to get to me. Everything from this point on rested on my word wizardry. And that was hardly an exaggeration. It was time to show off my linguistic techniques! To explain it in RPG terms, it was time to use all of my MP for a finishing move.

"Um . . . You know what? Your wings are really . . . nice. You're such a stylish . . . creature. A very high-level, fashionable monster! Um . . . whew. That should do it."

"Oh, you've done it alright! You're attacking my heart directly! How rude! I'm not a creature—and I'm not a monster, ryui!"

At least I'd gotten a reaction out of him—I hit him right in the heart!

I wasted all my MP in that final attack! But you know, come to think of it, I didn't really have much MP to start with, so I guess that wasn't very impressive. I was supposed to be a word wizard, but how much magic had I really pulled off? He was a pretty tough case!

"I'm an instructor that is assigned to care for special students, ryui. We'll be spending most of our time together, so we might as well be friends, ryui!"

"Hey, what do you mean by *special*?"

I hadn't even done anything weird yet and they were already treating me differently! Had they looked into my application's reference letters or something?

Thinking back on things, I guess I had run into a few problems with my homeroom teacher. My memories of those days came rushing back, fresh and sparkling, without any effort on my part, like I was dying and my life was flashing before my eyes. I couldn't stop it.

Whatever. I guess I couldn't blame them for wanting

to keep a closer eye on me. And besides, I'd always been the sort of person that would rather have people around than be stuck all alone.

"I guess you're a little cute, in your own way. Maybe you can be my mascot?"

"That's heartbreaking, so I'll pretend I didn't hear it, ryui."

Had I lost my ability to evaluate beauty? I wanted to walk around and ask the other people what they thought of him. Was Bimii actually cute or not?

On second thought, the result of that survey might upset Bimii, so I decided not to follow through. I'm such a nice person!

I kept my thoughts to myself, hummed a song, and kept walking to the dormitories. The campus was so large that I couldn't see the whole thing at once. Not only were there a lot of lectures halls and dormitories scattered around the grounds, there were also futuristic-looking shops here and there. The intention must have been to make sure the campus had everything necessary for our high school lives. As you might expect, the shops sold daily necessities and clothes. But I also passed movie theaters and some areas that looked like amusement parks.

"Wow! It's more like a city than a school campus!"

"You can shop right from that device of yours, ryui! When you participate in the battles, you earn points based on your performance. Those points can be used to shop here on campus, ryui!"

"What a weird system! How exciting! I love it!"

He was right. I took a peak into a store I was passing and, sure enough, the price of the products had been replaced with stickers indicating the necessary amount of points to purchase them. Of course, the more classy and luxurious items required more points to purchase and the daily necessities were on sale for a small amount of points. Hm . . . They'd really thought this all through!

But one thing about it bothered me. If you joined a club that wasn't successful in the battles, it meant that you would have very little money to live on while you were here. Were they trying to turn the campus into a Darwinian nightmare, where only the strong could survive!?

The campus was surrounded by mountains and covered in well-manicured gardens and trees. The campus was even better than the pamphlet had made it seem!

The overall impression I got was that the campus and academy were completely removed from reality. It wasn't just the strange welcome party I'd witnessed that made me feel that way.

It felt a little strange. It felt like I'd wandered into another world.

The dormitories themselves were built with large avenues and green spaces between them. The buildings were so unique that I didn't think I would ever get bored looking at them.

Once you learned your way around, it was the sort of place you couldn't get lost. Anyway, the place was so large and expansive that you could rent vehicles to get around. They were like electric snowboards, and of course, they were simple enough that you didn't need a license to drive one—perfect for young students like us.

"But you need points to rent them, ryui."

"Hm . . . it's a dog-eat-dog world."

It was like they were condemning members of weaker clubs to a pedestrian life. It's like they were saying that trash like us needed to walk. (Of course no one had actually *said* anything that bad.)

Maybe they designed it that way to encourage

everyone to do their best. Maybe that was the only way to get the students to take the battles seriously.

I'd always been into sports and competition, so I would probably fit in just fine. And yet . . .

"Why do they only have culture-themed clubs?"

"Because that's how the headmaster wants it. I mean, that's the official academy policy, ryui!"

"You mean whatever the headmaster wants becomes policy? If that's what baldy wants, then what kind of person is he?"

I had always assumed that headmasters had to be bald. It was an assumption of mine that I'd thought unassailable. I immediately pictured him that way. Did that mean that he liked his students quiet and submissive? But all the students I'd met so far looked like they were at least as active and aggressive as athletes.

The mysteries were only getting deeper.

*

"We made it! This is the dorm you've been assigned to, ryui!"

"Wow! It's so beautiful! It's like a castle from the middle ages!"

The building didn't look like a dorm at all. It was surrounded by thick castle-like walls. Maybe it was a security system to protect us, since it was an all-girls dorm?

I couldn't believe my luck. I'd always wanted to live in a place like this! Do me a favor and imagine heart-shaped bubbles floating around my head—just like a manga.

I was so excited! I remembered when I'd told my old classmates that the academy was going to be a boarding school. Some of them had said, "Ew! Mixed dorms? It's going to smell like sweaty socks!" I felt validated now. I wanted to run back and shove it in their faces.

The building definitely didn't look like it would smell like sweat—more likely it would smell like expensive perfume. I won! Victory is mine! Winners live in castles! The next time I go home, I'd have to brag about it. If I had to, I'd spend all night bragging about it!

I was so excited that my breath had grown ragged. After how hard I'd tried to be prim and proper, too! I was messing it up.

"Let me show you to your room, ryui!"

I held my device up to the auto-locking door, which swung open on its own after a series of beeps. Bimii flew in through the door as if it were the most ordinary thing in the world.

"Just a second . . ."

I grabbed him out of the air to stop him. Wasn't there something we had to be sure of first, something that we hadn't checked on yet?

The answer would have a significant impact on everything that would happen later. I was a maiden. My favorite food was salted beef tongue, but I was a maiden. On Valentine's Day, I morphed into a monster that ran around stealing chocolate from people, but I was a maiden. In the summers, sometimes I spied on the girl's swimming team, but I was a maiden. A MAIDEN! (I was starting to get out of breath.)

"Hey, um . . . Bimii? What kind of monster do you, um . . . like?"

"What kind of a question is that?"

I didn't want to ask him too directly, but I wasn't very good with euphemisms or at talking around things.

I just wanted to know if Bimii was male or female!

My plan was to figure out what kind monster he liked, and based on his answer, I could deduce whether Bimii was male or female. It was a perfect plan . . . I'm a genius, I know. Someone should give me an award.

"What kind of monster do I like? I've never thought about it, ryui. I guess it doesn't matter, ryui."

"You mean you can go either way? I didn't think you were such a free spirit!"

I assumed he was offering me an earth-shattering confession. I thought he was saying that he was attracted to both males and females.

Could it be? I hadn't expected to get an answer like that.

How was I supposed to treat him? Was I supposed to act differently now that I knew?

"I don't understand what you are so confused about, really. We're talking about monsters, right, ryui? If I had to pick, I guess I like big ones, ryui."

"How vulgar!"

"I don't understand anything that you're saying, ryui!"

My attempt to talk around the subject was only confusing him. I made up my mind and just asked him directly.

"If you wanted to know my sex, you could have just asked, ryui. Isn't it kind of weird to try and figure out what I am based on who I say I like? And besides, you've treated me like a monster up until now, ryui."

He was really surprised that I asked him and seemed really sad. I guess I really shouldn't have treated him like a monster.

"I'm sorry! I know that you aren't a monster! You're just a rare animal . . . A . . . rare treat?"

"Everything you're saying is so weird, ryui! Am I food now?"

I was going tell him that he looks like he'd be nasty and I wouldn't eat him, but he looked like he might start crying at any second, so I decided to let it go.

"This is the girl's dorm, isn't it? I know that you're an instructor, but I thought that it wouldn't be right for me to let you in if I didn't know you were male or female."

"So that's where this all came from. I'm just what I look like: a strapping male, ryui!"

He didn't really look like anything to me. I couldn't tell.

Thinking that there was really only one way to be

sure, I flipped Bimii over and looked at his hindquarters. He was screaming and protesting the whole time, but I didn't see anything down there that would make it clear either way. I squinted and looked closer. As far as I could tell, there wasn't anything there. Judging by his voice, I guess he sounded more like a male.

"But if you're a male, I shouldn't let you in here, should I? I know that you're an instructor, but there are rules of etiquette that I need to uphold here!"

I wasn't the sort of person that would lecture anyone on etiquette or manners. That's not the kind of girl that I was. But this was a girl's dormitory! I had to think about what was best for *everyone*!

"It's okay! I'm an adult, ryui! I would never look at a student that way, so you can set your mind at ease about that, ryui!"

"Adult?"

If he was an instructor, it was only natural that he'd be an adult. It was only natural, right? Was I the only one that had trouble accepting that? I guess he could be an adult. I mean, what did it really mean to be an adult, anyway? I was getting lost in adolescent philosophy again! Was I really supposed to believe that this crazy thing was an adult? I could hardly hold myself back from screaming at the top of my lungs. But no, I couldn't let him see how unnerved I was. I had to play it cool.

"Are you thinking rude things again, ryui?"

I guess I hadn't done a good job hiding my feelings. Some of it had leaked through. I wondered how much my face betrayed my private thoughts to others.

We were snapping at each other in the entrance to the dorms when someone came running over and chirped, "Hiiiii there, teacher! What are you doing here? Pretending to be an intruder? Pretending to be a monster?"

"I'm not a monster, ryui! Oh, if it isn't Himi-chan, the Calligraphy Club representative!"

It was my itty-bitty senpai, Himi Yasaka, from the welcome party. She came hopping over from the interior of the dormitory.

Whoa, I was so excited I could hardly contain myself. She was so cute. I just had to kidnap her! Bimii might have looked like the intruder here, but the truth was that *I* was the one with devious intentions!

Ermmm! Before I could stop myself, before I even knew what I was doing, I reflexively reached out and hugged her. I did it before even saying hello. I did it before even introducing myself! How was I supposed to hold myself back from her, from this charismatic Calligraphy Club representative, adorable senpai?

Ermmmmmmmm! She was like a cute little animal. She was like a cute little *stuffed* animal. And I hugged her close and picked her up. It was the sort of behavior that anyone would forgive me for. Even if I went to trial for it, the judge would just laugh and say, "Of course you'd have to hug her. Just look at her!" Anyone would forgive me for it. God himself would forgive me for it!

"Gyaaaaa! How cuuuute! So cute!"

I suddenly realized that I was shrieking like a stereotypical little girl. My voice was so high that I couldn't believe it came from my mouth. I sounded like a shrieking fan girl meeting her favorite movie star at the airport. Whenever I saw videos like that, I was always annoyed with them. But apparently, I had the capacity to be even worse. My audience, Bimii, must have been pretty annoyed with me, too.

"Ahhh . . . You're so small and cute! Do you live here? Are we going to live under the same roof? Are we? I'll give you carrots every day!"

I squeezed myself against her and rubbed my cheek against hers. Himi-chan pulled away from me, shouting, "I am not small! I'm 180 centimeters tall! Please don't treat me like a child! I'm a giant!"

No matter how you looked at her, she wasn't anywhere near 180 centimeters. And besides, if giants were only 180 centimeters, then the world would be full of them. Wouldn't that be terrifying?

"And we are *not* living together! And why would you think I want carrots every day? Does Himi look like a rabbit to you? Did you say that because someone told you I hate vegetables?"

Did you hear that? She referred to herself in the third person. Even though she's in high school! Even though she's my senpai? Third person!

She was a total angel. What to do!? I never thought I'd meet a real angel! Is this what happens to you if you don't eat vegetables? Do you turn into a cute, lovable girl? If so, maybe it was time for me to stop eating them.

"Okay. Understood, senpai. I mean, Himi-chan."

"What do you understand? Let me go!!"

She was screaming and shaking her head and trying to push me away, and honestly, I couldn't get enough of it. I wanted to get a video of her acting that way and play it on TV every night before I went to bed. It was so relaxing. Somebody, anybody, hurry and bring a video camera! Hurry!

"Eruna, you should probably let her go, ryui. No one will like you if you're annoying!"

"Right!"

Bimii was right, so I let her go. I raised both of my hands into the air, trying to prove that I wasn't touching her. (I might have been a little late to prove that.) My father had taught me that pose. He said it was what you had to do to prove that you weren't touching women on crowded trains. My father had a very difficult commute. I'd even seen him cry about it once. So I'm sorry, dad, but I used the pose you taught me, even though I really *had* been touching her. I let it go to waste. Although, thinking back on it now, I wondered why he'd felt the need to teach me that pose in the first place. Did he think I was going to be accused of molestation? What kind of girl did he take me for?

Anyway, I kept my hands up, trying to show that I didn't touch her. I really didn't want her to hate me! How would our beautiful love story ever get off the ground if she hated me from the start? Better not set off too many red flags.

"OW! You squeezed me so hard. It really hurt! Why are you so strong? Are you a sumo wrestler?"

"I'm so sorry. But hey, have you ever seen such a thin sumo wrestler?"

"Huh? I just meant that as a joke. Do you want to keep it going? Don't keep a joke going if you don't like it! Teacher! This girl is weird!"

She was making fun of me. This little demon was making fun of me! Oh well, I didn't hate it. Actually, it was getting me a little excited!

"Himi-chan, this is Eruna Ichinomiya, a new student, ryui. She's a little weird. She hasn't decided what club she wants to join yet. Keep an eye on her for me, will you, ryui? She *is* pretty strange."

How many times was he going to call me weird? Was Bimii trying to get revenge on me now? I wanted to put him in his place, but I couldn't do anything too sudden or violent in front of Himi-chan. Argh!

"Eruna-chan, right? I'm Himi Yasaka! I'm in the Calligraphy Club! Nice you meet you, weirdo!'"

"I'm not weird, but it's nice to meet you to, Himi-chan! Let's be friends . . . like, really close friends! Let's be so close that other people get confused about our relationship! What do you think?"

I hadn't planned on going off the rails again, but pretty soon I was panting and nearly out of breath. Not good! At this rate, she really would think I was weird!

"You certainly are energetic, Henna-chan*! Hey, Henna-chan, were you assigned to his building?"

"What do you mean, 'Henna-chan?' Are you calling me weird again? Is that a mix of 'hen' and my name? If so, why did you make sure to use all of 'hen' but just the 'na' from my name? You think I'm that weird?"

The worst part of it was that her nickname for me was pretty good. It was easy to say, easy to remember, and natural enough that I would probably instinctively respond if she called me by it.

"Heh, heh. I'm only joking!"

She seemed very at ease, even more relaxed and fun than I had expected when I first met her. How lovely! Himi Yasaka didn't have any faults at all!

Ding-ding! I imagined a sign flipping over and illuminating itself in the air next to her. It said "No Faults" and was written in steady cursive calligraphy.

I was happy I had decided to apply to the academy.

Any points that the institution had lost in my book, because of Shigure's presence, were more than made up for by Himi-chan.

Shigure would have broken down in tears had he heard my thoughts at the moment, but I was focusing all my energy on stopping myself from hugging Himi-chan again. It was nearly more than I could bear!

"Himi-chan, it seems that Eruna has been assigned to this dormitory, ryui."

Focused on controlling my compulsion to hug, Bimii stepped in and offered an explanation for my presence, to get the conversation going again.

The last thing I wanted was to be rescued by Bimii, but I had no choice for the time being. I'm sure it would be fine. He wouldn't betray me, would he?

"Oh, really? Then I'll show you to your room! All the members of the Calligraphy Club are housed in this building, so I know my way around pretty well. Let's be friends!"

Ta-da! Not only was I rescued and safe, I'd just won the lottery! My oh my, how one's fortune can turn on a dime.

I had to keep myself from freaking out, so I started

to bang my head against the wall. Ahaha! I could hardly contain my joy! But if I didn't control myself soon, I'd scare her off!

"Henna-chan, what are you doing? Are you trying to introduce yourself to the building? Is it something like the way sumo wrestlers greet each other? I'm confused."

"I wonder if you'll learn my real name any time soon? It's starting to bother me! And that sumo joke is starting to get old, too! Do I look like I'm introducing myself to a *building*?"

"Um . . ."

"Oh, and now you're not interested in talking anymore? Is that it? And by the way, this is NOT a sumo thing. And YOU, Bimii, stop acting like a sumo referee!"

Bimii was acting like Bimii, striking a pose as if he were calling a victor in a sumo match.

"Well, well, if Himi-chan says that she'll show us around, I think we should let her, ryui!"

He patted my shoulder as if he was trying to comfort or console me after a defeat—which was really obnoxious. Did he think I'd been pushed out of the ring? No, wait! This wasn't a sumo match! Argh!

I wanted to cradle my head in my hands and cry. My

brain had been converted into a sumo wrestler's brain! Hey, just what IS a sumo wrestler's brain?

"Okay then, come right this way! You're permitted to wear your shoes in the common areas of the building. Sometimes I forget that and I take my shoes off at the entrance! Haha! Anyway, come on in!"

Himi-chan trotted ahead to show us the way. Aww . . . she was like a little puppy!

How wonderful! How perfect! I could talk to her normally even though she was my senpai (which was great, because I'm not very good at speaking formally). She wasn't bad at all! She was so friendly! She was so nice that she was already showing me around. We'd only just met a few minutes ago! Her tiny little body was hidden away inside that hakama of hers, which was really, um . . . exciting.

Bimii whispered to me, "Eruna, I can hear you again, ryui. I can hear everything you are saying about her, ryui."

"Shut up and leave me alone. Just go treat yourself to a chanko nabe* or something."

"Still on the sumo thing, ryui?"

While I stood there arguing with Bimii, Himi-chan

had managed to pull ahead of us. She poked her head out from the stairwell and called to us from the second floor.

"Heeey! Follow me!"

She was trying to rush us along. Oh boy! She could rush me along any day of the week. I could picture it now. She'd shake me awake and rush me along with that cute voice of hers. "Wake up! Wake up!" And she'd think I was fast asleep, but really I'd snap up at a 90-degree angle, when she was only halfway through her sentence, and say, "Good morning!" Then she'd try to rush me along again, saying, "Hurry up and go to the bathroom!" And she'd be so convincing that, even though I might be constipated, everything would turn out smoothly in the end. I bet that she'd only get to "hurry up and go . . ." before my maidenly anxieties evaporated, and I'd go to the bathroom, chipper as ever. And then if she tried to hurry me, I wouldn't understand what she wanted, and I'd just bark, "Woof!" And she'd say, "Turn around three times and then bark!" But I'd turn around hundreds of times and then fall into her lap on purpose. That would be the life—rushed by Himi-chan, forever, until the day I died. Wait. What was I saying? Had my imagination gotten the better of me again!?

"Okay! Just a second! We're on our way!"

I was drowning in the ocean of my overactive imagination and I had just answered without ever snapping back to reality. I figured that, if I showed enough enthusiasm, there wouldn't be a problem, but . . .

I looked around the interior of the dormitory. The exterior had looked like a castle, but the interior was so gorgeous and ornate that it definitely stood up to whatever expectations the building's facade had sparked. The rooms were enormous. The ceilings were so high that it was almost hard to believe they let students live there.

We were still near the entrance, so there were always students passing by as they came and went. They almost all stopped and bowed politely to Bimii, which felt very surreal. Everyone really treated the . . . creature . . . like a normal instructor.

Himi-chan had also called him teacher, so I was starting to wonder if I'd made a mistake by making fun of him this whole time. What had I gotten myself into? I stared at his face for a while, trying to figure it out.

"What's wrong, ryui?"

"Um . . . I still think your face is a little weird. It's like God kind of messed up the design a little bit, don't you think? Like maybe his hand slipped? Or maybe he was blindfolded when he put you together?"

"You're so rude, ryui!"

Well, I'd reconfirmed my suspicions. Bimii was the sort of creature that practically begged to be made fun of. I made up my mind to continue treating him as I had been. After all, first impressions are important, right? Better not be a flip-flopper, right? Don't mind me, Bimii! I've been burdened with too heavy a task! Hey now . . . heavy?

"Sorry, Heavy . . . Himi-chan is calling for us. We better go!"

"Did you just change my name, ryui? What's it supposed to mean? Is it 'heavy' as in how serious something is? Or are you keeping that sumo joke going? What are you trying to say, ryui? Are you punishing me for finally choking back my tears and accepting the name 'Bimii?'"

He seemed to be really taken aback. I was certainly not trying to keep the sumo joke going, so he was definitely overthinking it. I wasn't the sort of girl to keep harping on a lame joke!

I laughed it off and finally relaxed. Bimii calmed down a bit, too. He'd been flapping around the room anxiously, then sighed and settled onto my shoulder. I pet him softly and started to climb the steps.

The stairway was so large that ten people could have lined up across it without touching. Sure, there were probably a lot of students that lived in the building, but even considering that, the furnishings seemed more opulent than necessary.

The school was private, but my mother had been pleasantly surprised at how reasonable the tuition and boarding fees were. It made me wonder how on earth the academy had enough money to build such fancy dorms.

I slapped the walls with my palm and thought about it as I climbed the steps. But I couldn't think about it for long, because Himi-chan was calling to me from the top and motioning for me to follow her. I couldn't resist!

"Here I come, Himi-chan! Mu-wah!"

I ran up the stairs like lightning, but then . . .

"Here you are, Eruna-chan! This is your room!"

She was standing there motioning to the empty hallway extending from the top of the stairs. None of the doors lining the hallway were open. I was very confused about what she was trying to tell me.

"Huh? What?"

I had no idea what she wanted to say. There were two sleeping bags thrown on the floor at the end of the hallway. One of them was puffed up. It looked like someone was already inside of it.

Uh, maybe it was a joke? I didn't know how to respond. Should I laugh? It was just a sleeping bag lying there on the ground! I had to watch out. I had almost taken her seriously.

"Okay, so we're still joking around, are we? So where is my room, really? Is it on the second floor? Or do we need to keep climbing the stairs?"

I looked up the stairway to see that it seemed to have no end. Just how many stories did this dormitory have?

"What do you mean, 'joking around?' This is it! This is where you'll be living from now on," Himi-chan said, stone faced. She pointed to the empty sleeping bag.

"This is my room? My room is a sleeping bag?"

"It sure is! He-he!"

"I'm supposed to come back to this sleeping bag to

reflect on my long days at the academy? Really? Even if they were great days, that might make me suicidal!"

"It will be fine! These sleeping bags are really warm!"

"It might warm up my body, but what good is it if my heart is freezing!? Look! Whoever is in that bag there is shaking a little! They must be crying themselves to sleep!"

I could even hear a little voice on the air, whispering, "I want to go home. I want to go home!"

What sort of tragedy was I witnessing? Was it some kind hazing ritual for the new students? Could anyone actually be so cruel?

"Didn't you hear that the rooms are divvied up based on the outcome of the club battles?"

Bimii had explained that to me back at the welcome party. I had been pretty shocked by it, so of course I still remembered it clearly. The battles were scheduled for certain times throughout the term. The clubs were ranked based on their performances. The rankings were very important and were used to determine the students' rooms, meals, and all the important parts of their campus lives.

"But! But I just got here today!"

They couldn't have actually been suggesting that everyone had to start out this way, could they? At that exact moment, I could even see other new students with big smiles on their faces moving their luggage into nice rooms. I was shocked. Bimii spoke up after noticing my indignant expression.

"It's because you were so late getting here, ryui! Everyone else managed to decide what club they wanted to join back before the party, ryui. That's why they already have assigned rooms, ryui!"

Bimii put on his serious instructor face and spoke very sternly, as if he were chastising me.

"That's right. All the students that moved up from Mikagura Middle School have definitely already decided what club they are joining. Anyone that hasn't decided what club they are joining by now is in the minority—it's very rare! As you can see, though, you're not the only one," Himi-chan said, pointing to the other sleeping bag lined up next to mine. I didn't know what kind of person was inside of it, but I had a feeling that we were going to be friends.

"I get it now. So this is the type of academy that makes undecided kids sleep in the hallway. But if you pick a club then you get to have a room, right?"

"Oh, and by the way, students that haven't joined a club are only provided with one meal a day."

"Won't that kill you!? Hey! Don't people die if they don't eat!?"

That was ridiculous. There had to be a limit to the insanity!

Why did the academy want its students to join clubs so badly?

And even if they did, why not give us enough time to make up our minds?

I was still reeling from these crazy revelations when Himi-chan went over and poked the sleeping bag to encourage whoever was inside to come out.

"Heeeey! Come on out! You can always join my Calligraphy Club! We have really big rooms and really yummy food!"

The sleeping bag stopped shaking and listened to what Himi-chan was saying. Obviously, I was listening closely, too.

That meant if I just decided to join the Calligraphy Club, I could avoid all these problems, right? Isn't that what she was saying?

I didn't really have any experience with calligraphy, aside from a couple of lessons I had to take back in elementary school. If I remember correctly, the assignment had been to write down my dreams for the future. I'd written "gold prospector," and my teacher had not been pleased and gave me a very low score.

I cried and asked her why she had to stomp on the dreams of a child. She just said, "The problem isn't your answer. It's your calligraphy—it's terrible." I felt betrayed and destroyed. It was very embarrassing.

I just didn't have very good handwriting. That's all! There was nothing wrong with me as a person. All I had to do was practice, right? Maybe, if I joined the Calligraphy Club, it would give me the practice I needed to improve anyway. Maybe I just needed to go "prospecting" for my "buried talent," eh? (I'm pretty satisfied with that one.)

Whoever was in the sleeping bag ignored me and said, "Um . . . Can I join the Calligraphy Club then? I don't really have any experience."

She crawled out of the sleeping bag and tried to look as weak and pathetic as she could. She had long pink hair pulled back into three pigtails. I couldn't help but notice her downturned, sad-looking eyes. She was very beautiful.

"What? But I want to join the Calligraphy Club, too! I figured no one can hold me down as long as I dedicate myself to getting better!"

I raised my hand in the air and yelled that I wanted to join, pressing myself forward obnoxiously to make sure I was heard. I couldn't officially join the club there, which meant I'd have to sleep in the sleeping bag for the night, in the hallway, with everyone walking by me. I could see it now. The mean kids would kick me on their way by and say, "Oh, I just didn't see you there." The girls would step on me with their little feet. I guess that part wouldn't be so bad. They might sit on me and then say, "Oh, I thought this was a beanbag! I didn't realize there was a person in there! Sorry!" Actually, that wouldn't be so bad either. They'd put their cute little butts directly on me!

Wait, no! I was getting distracted again! I didn't want to sleep in a bag in the hallway! No way!

"Okay, then I'll give you both an easy test to enter the club. It's just a formality. It's really easy, so don't you worryyyyy!"

She passed us both brushes and a little pot of ink. She also gave us some nice paper to write on. All we had to do was write down a character that we liked.

"You don't have to have experience! No problem at all! Calligraphy isn't about technique anyway. It's about how much feeling you can express on the paper!" she smiled and explained to us.

Well, that didn't sound so bad, did it? With a test like that, I might even have a chance. If I really put my heart into it, it might even be something I'm good at.

After all, I had grown a lot since my elementary school days.

I decided that it would be unwise to attempt a hard phrase like "gold prospector" again. If I could write whatever I wanted, then I'd have the best chance of success. That is to say, if I went with characters I was used to writing, I'd probably do much better.

My brush slid smoothly over the surface of the paper. I hadn't tried my hand at calligraphy in a very long time. It was kind of fun! Maybe I really WAS suited for the Calligraphy Club!

I tried to look at what the girl next to me was writing.

"For an amateur, you're actually writing very well!

But the words you chose are a little too easy, no? Himi-chan said that calligraphy is all about pouring out your heart, so maybe you shouldn't hold back so much!"

"Um . . . maybe . . ."

The girl from the sleeping bag took a look at my masterpiece. A confused look washed over her face. Ha! She must have been shocked at how superior my work was to her own! For a second, I thought I could hear her heart breaking.

"Are you done? Okay! Let's start with yours, shall we?" Himi-chan said, talking to the sleeping bag girl.

"Oh, alright." She shut her eyes tightly and passed the paper to Himi-chan, embarrassed—so cute.

Girls are the best! Girls, banzai! I'm a girl, too!

Himi-chan nodded and smiled while she looked over the girl's work. "'Spring,' right? Not the most creative choice, but the shape is lovely. You can really feel the expectation for change inherent in the shape! And your brush movements here—just lovely! You passed!"

She said it so easily! I thought there would be a higher bar set for club admission. I guess she had said it would be easy. Was it just a formality?

"Oh, yay! Thank you so much! I'll do my best to make your club proud!"

The sleeping bag girl was very excited, just because she'd passed a simple test. How cute! I wanted to give her a big kiss!

"Himi-chan, it's my turn, right? I'm really proud of how it turned out. Here, have a look!"

"Okay! Show it to me! Um . . . what's this?"

Maybe my lines were too expressive for her to see the characters they formed. I watched her eyes flit over the paper. They grew wider and more confused the closer she appeared to look.

"What . . . Um . . . What did you try to write there, ryui?" Bimii asked, unable to contain himself.

To think that I was capable of creating such a shocking piece of work with so little effort! I must have been really special.

"Um, this is kind of hard to say, but the handwriting is so bad I can't tell what you were trying to write."

"Honestly, I'm having a hard time with it, too. Is it supposed to be Japanese? I told you to express yourself—is that what you've done here? Just how much darkness do you have inside?"

That sleeping bag girl was meaner than I'd expected.

"It just looks like a big black blob, ryui!"

I was expecting a storm of compliments, not a storm of insults! Was it really that bad? Were my aesthetic leanings too obscure for them? Was I the sort of artist that only earns respect after they die!?

"I believe that calligraphy is about the SOUL, not about how perfect your handwriting is! Am I wrong!?"

"There's a limit to everything. Sorry, Eruna, but we can't accept you into the club! As for you, sleeping bag girl, you're welcome to join us in the club dorm rooms tonight!"

They turned and looked like they were going to abandon me, leaving me wringing my hands in the hallway. I thought I'd never seen anything so sad in all my life! I couldn't get them to take me, too. I was left with my calligraphy. Bimii settled down next to me and tried to comfort me, but it was hard to ignore the stark contrast between the smiling girls in the Calligraphy Club and myself, all alone.

"Okay, well, I'll send the official form later. Can you tell me your name and what class you're in? Actually, I don't want to forget anything, so please write it down, right here!"

"Understood. And I'm so glad to be out of the sleeping bag! My last name is Katai. I'd like to be addressed that way. It's written with the characters for 'flower' and 'bag.'"

She explained her name as she wrote it on a sheet of paper in charming, round letters.

"So I guess we should have called you 'Flower Bag' instead of 'Sleeping Bag!' Well, we were pretty close anyway. What a gorgeous name!"

Who would have thought that a person's name would affect the way you viewed them so dramatically? She suddenly looked beautiful! A woman can really shine when she leaves a sleeping bag in the hall for the comfort and security of the Calligraphy Club rooms!

So then, what did I look like? I was going to have to spend the night curled up on the hallway floor! My only other companion—gone! If I was going to have to live this way, I would have written something else! It might be too long. I could have gone with the theme of an essay I'd written in middle school: *My teacher realized she was over the hill and devoted herself to becoming a beautiful witch.* I could have been really expressive with that!

"The problem was with your handwriting, not with what you wrote, ryui. Also, if you have to walk the streets at night, you should keep an eye out for that teacher of yours. You wouldn't want to be attacked, ryui."

He had a good point. I remembered that teacher telling me, when she played video games, she named the computer players after me, designed their avatars to look like me, and set their AI and strength to the weakest setting. That was how she practiced.

What a gloomy person! No wonder she never got married! I told her how I felt, and she spent the weekend in her apartment, working out with a punching bag that she'd taped my face onto.

In hindsight, I should probably have been grateful that she never attacked me directly. The more I thought about it, the scarier it got.

"Bye, Eruna-chan! We're going to get going. I hope that you find a club that works for you! If you have any trouble, you can always talk to me, mkay?"

"I'm having trouble right now! How could I be in worse trouble than this? You're leaving me alone to sleep on the floor of the hallway!"

Did I have to eat here, too? Was I supposed to eat

my meals kneeling in the hallway? What if my legs fell asleep when I was eating? Would anyone come to poke them, prompting me to yell, "Hey, stop that!" Or would I just have to whisper to myself, "Ow, my leg fell asleep. How sad! How lonely!"

"Ahaha! Oh, Eruna, you're always joking! See you later!"

"I'm not joking. I'm serious! And what do you mean 'see you later?' You're not coming back?"

They made to leave, so I rushed to block their way down the hall. Throwing my arms out wide, I furiously shook my head.

"Um, I think we're in the same class, so I'll see you soon!"

"Katai-chan, how can you betray me like this? You get out of your sleeping bag, and then you smile as you leave me to mine? How do you live with yourself!?"

When I'd first found her, she was shivering inside her sleeping bag, afraid to even show her face. Now she was skipping down the hall like a butterfly emerged from its cocoon? It felt like she was condescending to me, like she wanted to say, "Sleeping bag? Oh, I moved into a real bed a long time ago! Sleeping bags . . .

they're so smelly, aren't they?" Was I just imagining her condescension?

Her droopy eyes looked perkier then they had. People change so easily, don't they? The horror!

I spread my arms and legs as wide as I could, but unfortunately, the hallway was too wide to cover effectively. They walked by me easily.

"You can use the sleeping bag I was just in, if you want. It should be nice and warm!"

"I don't need your pity! It will only make me long for the warmth of another person! How can you leave me alone here? You backstabber!"

My voice echoed pathetically down the hall. Himi-chan nodded to Bimii, and Katai-chan made a small apologetic gesture. The two of them left me there to fend for myself.

I heard the din of far-off excitement carrying through the floor and walls. It rang in my ears sentimentally.

It . . . It wasn't supposed to be like this! I'd used that phrase before, at the welcome party, but it came tumbling out of my mouth again.

Seriously—who would expect, when they were on their way to their dorm room, I would be assigned to a sleeping bag in the hallway? No one, that's who! The most pessimistic person in the world wouldn't have been able to predict this hellish predicament!

It's not like I thought I deserved the most lavish and elegant room in the building. I'm not so selfish. Sure, I'd thought about sharing a room with a cute girl and spending my days in a pink, feverish haze. But all I really wanted was a nice roommate in a room with a bunk bed. She'd sleep on the bottom bunk, and I'd be on the top. When she fell asleep, I'd look down on her sleeping face and think about how lucky I was. And so what if I'd also thought about taking a bath with her and helping her get all washed up and clean? It's just a little fun, right? Just some good, clean, Eruna-style fun. Right?

I couldn't believe that things would go this way. I took a Lupin III-style dive into my sleeping bag and sighed.

"Okay, I'm going to head back to my room, ryui. I'll come pick you up in the morning, ryui."

"What!? Are you seriously about to leave me here by myself? Just when I was starting to think you might be a good monster? Just when I thought you were blossoming into the sort of monster that looked on admiringly as we humans go about our tasks, you look at me like with that look in your eyes, like you just know we are going to be best friends?"

"I think it's just about time you stopped treating me like a monster, ryui! I'd like to look on as you blossom into the kind of person who treats me nicely, ryui!"

It was hard to tell just how much our exchange had upset him. He narrowed his eyes and avoided the gaze of the other passing students as he flew out of the hallway, a blank look on his face.

Finally left all alone, I crawled into my sleeping bag—not caring that my uniform would get wrinkled—and looked up at the high ceiling. I'd been so lucky. I'd met someone that I could get into a real shouting match with.

I had my family back at home. Sure, I had my own room to escape to, but we normally spent most of our time together in the living room, yelling about something or another. I always had friends at my side back at my old school. I was the sort of person that could be friends with boys and girls equally. Even after changing classes, I normally found myself gravitating toward the center of attention. Thinking back on those days, it struck me that I was probably only alone when I went to bed at night.

I guess these things had to happen from time to time. By tomorrow, classes will start and I'll be out there making friends. I'm sure I'd learn a lot about all the different clubs, too.

Considering how strange the academy had already proven itself to be, I was sure that the coming days would be jam-packed with excitement.

What sort of friends would I make? What sort of teachers would I have? What would their classes be like? The more I let myself imagine it, the faster time flew by. By the time I thought to look out the window, it was already well past sunset. I burrowed deeper into my sleeping bag and shut my eyes.

"Aawwwwn. I'm hungry . . . And I want a shower. . . but more than anything else . . ."

I couldn't wait for the next day!

I think I had a very long dream that night. My homeroom teacher back in middle school was there.

(She was a single, 27-year-old woman that constantly asked her students how old she looked, and she would explode if you didn't give a number lower than her actual age. If you said she looked like a college student, she would sing and dance by herself.) She was trying to encourage me to move forward.

"You can do it, Eruna Ichinomiya. I believe in you."

"T . . . Teacher!"

"You'll meet great people, gain tons of experience points, and get your hands on the very best treasure."

"Yes. Yes!"

"You'll break into someone's house and open their dresser without permission. You'll eat a rare seed and get mad that it only raised your stats by one. You'll be the cute girl character, so your equipment will all be very scanty."

"What are you talking about? Am I in an RPG now? I thought you were trying to encourage me, but you were just talking about a game! Is that it?"

"ANYWAY."

"Yes? 'Anyway' what?"

"You can ignore the demon king for now. Focus your efforts on finding the youth-restoring potion and then bring it to me! As quickly as you can! Hurry! Before it's too late!"

"What are you talking about now? I thought you were going to start crying a second ago. How are you giving me orders?"

The dream went on like that for a while. What did I care? I had already left that school. They'd dumped salt all over me when I left the building. Ugh! Now I wanted to call that teacher and tell her that it was already too late! But if I did that, I could picture her forcing her way into Mikagura (even though trespassing was strictly forbidden) to slap me.

Maybe I was lucky to have had that dream. For the first time in my life, I got a great night of sleep. I didn't wake up once.

"Ummm, I was just about to conquer the elf village and declare myself the uncontested victor in the battle for . . ."

I guess I was still dreaming about the RPG when I raised myself from the bag. Just when I was muttering my plans for domination, a student stumbled by and overheard me. They screamed, apparently terrified for their lives, and ran away. Oh well, things could be worse.

And so my first day at the academy was a raucous action-packed extravaganza. The day ended just as it had begun: hectic and confusing.

Movement Three: School Life in a Sleeping Bag

Sweat poured down my face. Bimii flew ahead and told me where to go. I ran after him, across the early morning campus.

"Ah, what a nice morning! I don't see any other students out and about though. Did I wake up a little late again?"

"Not 'a little late,' ryui! Classes will be starting any second now, ryui!"

Yup, that's pretty much what I'd figured. I hadn't seen a single student since I left the building.

I tried to avoid the obvious by suggesting that, maybe, I'd actually gotten up too early, but the hands on the clock were merciless in their condemnation.

"Hey, I learned a spell to turn back time a while ago. Should I try it out?"

"I know you just woke up, but do you think you're still in an RPG? Snap out of it! There's no such thing as magic, ryui! Come back to reality, ryui!"

My fantasies melted away when Bimii reprimanded me. Considering that he looked like he'd been pulled directly out of a fantasy novel himself, his argument wasn't very convincing. I mean, look at his wings and everything. He was flying!

According to him, he'd woken me up at a decent hour and led me to the shower room, then to the cafeteria for breakfast. The only problem was that I didn't remember any of it happening.

I wasn't hungry, and my hair was clean and brushed as if I really had taken a shower. I must have been half asleep the whole time, going through the motions unconsciously. If you stop to think about it, I was pretty impressive. If I could keep that kind of performance up, maybe I could even sleep through my classes!

"What's this? Some breakfast is still stuck to my cheek? Slurp! What is this stuff? Red elixir?"

"Are you still stuck in RPG mode? It's just ketchup, ryui! Is that what you think elixirs taste like? Stop talking. You're ruining the way I think about RPGs. You're even worse in the morning than I thought, ryui!"

My dream had been a pretty epic game-like story. I was clearly having trouble adjusting to reality again. I wonder what I had to do to keep the same dream going when I went to sleep that night? Saving systems sure were convenient, but there hadn't been one in my dream.

I slapped my own cheek to try and wake myself up. The sky above was exceptionally blue, and there wasn't a cloud to be seen. The sun was really beating down on me, which is why I was sweating so much.

I could just make out the main building where it stood over the horizon. The building itself was very large, which made it difficult to judge the distance to it.

The path I was running on was beautifully manicured, far more than necessary, which made running a breeze. The campus was just too large. I thought about renting one of those electric snowboard-type machines, but you needed points to do that, and I didn't have any yet.

Again, it was achingly clear that I needed to join a club as soon as possible.

"Whew."

I braced myself, then started running faster. I found myself wishing I had an airship—I must not have fully shaken my RPG mood. Bimii was clearly annoyed and kept pushing for me to run faster. So I did.

I slipped into the lecture hall just as the bell was

indicating the start of class. With the final reverberations of the chime, I burst into the room and ran for my seat. Everyone's eyes were locked onto me. For better or worse, over the years, I'd gotten used to being the center of attention. I cleared my throat loudly, as if to pretend that everything was normal, and took my seat.

When I was sitting and a bit calmer, the first thing that struck me as bizarre was how little interest my classmates had in Bimii, considering that he was such a strange creature.

But it wasn't that they were ignoring him. Some of them were clearly greeting him with their eyes. I couldn't wrap my mind around how they could all think he was normal.

"A lot of these kids graduated from Mikagura Middle School, so they are used to seeing instructors like me, ryui."

"Ooooh. I guess that makes sense."

Again, he must have known what I was thinking from the look on my face, because he immediately explained what I had wanted to know.

The talk of the middle school reminded me of the boy I'd met at the welcome party, Asuhi Imizu. Now I knew they had the same battle system back at Mikagura Middle School, too. Students like me—students completely unfamiliar with the way things were done at the academy—were a rarity.

That must have been why I was alone when I took the entrance exam.

When the room had calmed down from my dramatic entrance, I started to look around at the lecture hall. It was actually a very normal room—nothing stood out as particularly strange in any way.

Many of the students were not wearing their school uniforms, but rather uniforms that appeared to be based on the club they were in. A lot of them were carrying large items that clearly had no utility for the class. They were probably used in the club battles. The whole scene brimmed with freedom.

The room was less like a typical high school classroom and more like the sort of large university lecture halls that you see on TV or in movies.

"There are no assigned seats, so you can sit wherever you like, ryui."

"Neat! No assigned seats!"

I was a little sad that I'd miss out on those occasional

seating rearrangements (those are always so much fun), but I had to move on. I was in high school! I'd long moved beyond the time when it would be appropriate to shout for joy at a seat change. I was a young woman now!

"I don't think young women wake up shouting, 'Why should I save a world that won't let me marry as many princesses as I want!?' ryui."

"I said sorry! I can't help it if that's how my dream was going when I woke up."

The more accurately I remembered my dreams, the more I had to be ashamed of.

I heard excited conversation coming from the center of the room, where a clump of students had formed. I looked at them all. None of them appeared to have a special instructor assigned to them the way I did.

Did they really think I was going to cause problems for the academy? Was I that bad? Granted, no one had ever called me a model student, but I was always called happy and healthy in the past. I wasn't sure what they meant by 'happy and healthy' though. Maybe it wasn't supposed to be a compliment.

I didn't want to be treated differently than everyone

else! Ugh! Just thinking about it was starting to bum me out.

I had to repent for my past misdeeds. I could feel it. I tried to think of something to repent for, but the ideas came in a torrential downpour. I couldn't even hope to keep track of them all. Just when I was wondering where to start, the automatic door to the lecture hall slid open silently and the teacher entered the room on clacking high heels.

"Huh? Am I crazy? I feel like I've seen her somewhere before."

"You're not crazy. You've met Kurumi-sensei three times now, ryui! She even drove you here yesterday morning."

What? Did he mean . . . That was the same person? She was going to be my homeroom teacher?

I looked her over very carefully, from her head to her toes, taking the time to absorb every detail. Her hairstyle hadn't changed. Her glasses and makeup were a little different than they had been, but it was clear that she was the same person.

And she was still wearing that maid outfit. And she was so relaxed that her eyes almost made her look like she was sleepwalking—clearly she lived in her own world. I wonder what kind of things she liked? Her cold, disinterested gaze made me all the more curious.

"Kurumi-san!? From the entrance exam? Your real name was Kurumi!? I had no idea. It's like . . . It's like I had no idea how to answer a test question, so I just guessed and was RIGHT! Yay! But to tell the truth, I actually DID know. You see, I have these ESP-like powers. I'm really your classic psychic super girl. I knew! I knew Kurumi-sensei!"

"Eruna, you don't want to be so quick to rush out an explanation. You might get yourself in trouble, ryui."

"Sorry. I just thought it would be nice if people paid attention to me, considering how I've come to a new school where I don't know anyone at all. I just wanted people to look at me with an inkling of respect, you know? I thought that maybe if I had psychic powers, that would be my opportunity . . . Oh no, I'm so ashamed . . ."

"If you keep acting so pathetic, people will pay attention to you alright, but it won't be in the way that you want, ryui. Let's go back to the drawing board about your high school debut, okay? Let's really think it through, ryui!"

He was right. If I went with the psychic character I was creating, people would be more likely to whisper about me behind my back than they would be to surround me with warmth and encouragement. People probably wouldn't want to sit down and eat lunch with me. I'd end up eating all alone in an empty classroom somewhere. I'd just sit there, eating my eggs and telling myself that I would have to endure solitude, because of my exceptional abilities. *Exceptional* abilities— that's right. I had all the unwarranted confidence of a 15 year old. Besides, if I did have some special powers, I wouldn't stand out all that much in a place like this, especially considering the things I'd seen at the welcome party.

I'd seen battles there that unfolded like fantasy movies. They were more game-like than the RPG dream I'd been having! The whole school felt very unreal at times.

Anyway, Kurumi-san looked like she was the same age as me. How old was she really!? Did she really have her teaching license? Was she teaching illegally!?

Maybe everyone was just excited by their new lives at the academy. Or maybe her maid outfit was throwing everyone off, but the room still seemed to be simmering with conversation. She paid no mind to what was happening in the room but calmly let her eyes slide down to the device in her hand. It was displaying something like an attendance sheet.

"I will be your teacher this year. My name is Kurumi Narumi. This is my first year teaching, so I'm a little nervous. But I'm sure we will all be good friends in no time. Please call me Kurumi."

She said that she was nervous, but she certainly didn't seem like it. She stood there emanating coolness and telling us that we were going to be friends. She wanted us to call her by her first name!

What if she was like my old teacher in middle school, who was WAY too interested in herself? Was it my eternal fate to have teachers like that!?

Everyone in the room was impressed by her attitude and sense of power and authority—the whole room fell silent. Or so I thought, when . . .

"Kurumiiiiii!"

There were still girls that were so impressed with her that they jumped from their seats, hearts floating around their heads, and shouted with joy.

"You said girls, but you're the only one, ryui."

"What? Just me? The only one? The one and only?"

I had to start paying more attention. If I jumped out of my seat and fell over, then I'd really be the only one—the only one eating my lunch alone. That was the start of my Chuunibyou. Just thinking about it was terrifying.

I must have been overexcited, because the rest of the class, despite bathing in Kurumi-sensei's special aura, didn't seem to care one way or the other. The girl I'd met in the sleeping bag yesterday, Katai-chan, was there in the room, too. She didn't even cast a glance in my direction. It was kind of sad.

The teacher walked quietly toward the center of the room.

"Because this is the first day of class, I'd like to start with some introductions. We will go in order, based on your student number, starting with Eruna Ichinomiya."

"I . . . I have seat number one? Really? Aren't there any Abels or Arthurs or Alices in this class?"

"Are you still stuck on that RPG dream? None of the students here have sword-and-sorcery-style names, ryui! Drop the RPG thing. Really! Ryui!"

Oh, I guess I was still stuck in the middle of my RPG

adventure. I'm such a dreamer, aren't I?

I'd never been the first name on a class list before. Never! It was a novel experience. There was normally an Aoki-san or an Aikawa-san before me. I had my own way of getting through life. It consisted of using the people before me like a shield! I just had to stay safely behind them and not mess it up! Where are you, Aoki!? Aikawa!?

"They probably moved on to a normal high school, ryui."

I wasn't the sharpest person in the world. I had realized that Mikagura was not normal pretty quickly. But Bimii was an instructor there. He shouldn't say things like that out in public.

I was the first person in class to introduce herself. The burden was too heavy—the hurdle too high! If I could just go second, at least I would have been able to base my introduction on what the previous person had said. It couldn't be too long or too short. I had to add just enough humor to leave the audience feeling light and happy.

But that was impossible if I had to go first! What level of excitement should I aim for? What if I messed up?

The next student would be introduced and encouraged to make up for my mistakes. That would be so awkward! I couldn't let that happen—I'd rather die! What to do!?

Maybe it would be best to start off with a joke about my name? I could say, "My name is Euruna MaxNEET* Ichinomiya!" I wonder if a funny middle name like that would go over well with the class. No! That wouldn't work at all! What if "MaxNEET" stuck in their heads and the whole school started addressing me as MaxNEET-san? I could see it now: the whole school would spend three weeks laughing at me and treating me like a NEET. I couldn't stand the thought of it! People that didn't know me personally would say things like, "Why do they call you MaxNEET? Are you trying to be a NEET? Are you planning on dropping out? If you need someone to talk to, I'm here to listen." I couldn't handle being treated like that every day. I had to nail this introduction. I just sort of liked the sound of MaxNEET when I thought of it. But if I wasn't careful, I was going to condemn myself to weeks of careful explanatory follow-up conversations. I don't think my soul could bear it! The weight of it all would crush me like a pancake!

My mind ran in feverish circles, searching for just the right tone. All I came up with were things that would trip me up later.

"I don't think I even know what it really *means* to introduce yourself. I mean, when you really think about it, what *am* I? Why was I born? What do I live for?"

"Eruna, I think you're confusing yourself, ryui!"

I knew that—I knew I was overthinking it! But I'd already spent so much time thinking things over that everyone was staring at me. Kurumi-sensei was giving off a hurry-it-up vibe, too. What was I supposed to do?

"I get it. Leave it up to me, ryui! I'll take care of everything! I'm going to send an introduction speech to your device, ryui. All you need to do is read it loud enough for everyone to hear, ryui."

"Thank you, Bimii. I'll treat you to some raw meat later!"

"I'm not a monster, so I don't eat raw meat, ryui! At least cook it for me! I'll eat it after it's cooked and seasoned properly, ryui!"

My neural circuitry was on the verge of shorting out, so it would be a big help if he just told me what to say. I couldn't keep the class waiting any longer. He had to hurry. Hurry up, Bimii!

I cleared my throat loudly to buy some time as I waited for Bimii's speech to arrive. A second later, my device alerted me that I had a message. The name in the "from" field of the email was long and so fantastical that at first I couldn't read it. I had no idea who had messaged me—then I remembered that Bimii wasn't his real name. It was just something I'd come up with. I think he'd been upset and insisted that his real name was way better. It was too late for that—Bimii was Bimii. (That sounds like I have his character in mind, but I don't. I just can't be bothered with trying to learn his real name!)

I squinted at the screen, trying to figure out what it said. He had even included some directions for how to best enunciate and what parts to emphasize. He'd done a great job! If there were a test to tell me exactly how to deliver my introduction, I'd give him 100 points. A+.

"Go ahead, Ichinomiya-san."

She suggested I begin at the exact moment I felt ready to proceed. Full speed ahead, non-stop! No one can stop me! Here. I. Go, go, go!

All the eyes in the room were on me. I took a quick glance at the device in my hand and followed its direction. Brimming with confidence, I placed one foot on the desktop and loudly proclaimed, "To inject life into a stagnant battle culture, I've arrived from outside the system—I'm unaffiliated with any clubs. I'm Eruna Ichinomiya, the trick star of Mikagura Academy! When it comes to firsts, I'll top more lists than the attendance sheet. If you want to taste sweet victory, you'll beg me to join your club! Nice to meet you!"

I delivered the whole speech without stopping to breathe.

The room was so quiet that it hurt my ears.

Huh? Something was weird. What were they saying about me?

"Eruna is so cool! She's proclaimed herself the eye of the storm—the storm of battle, ryui! This feels like the start of a legend!"

He said it felt like the start of legend. I thought it felt like the end of my academic career. Was I just imagining things?

I should never have put my faith in Bimii. I mean—I mean—Come on, just think about it! Was I really so desperate that I had to grasp at straws like that?

I didn't let myself get angry. I just slowly sat down

again in silence. I felt more like a *slip* star than a *trick* star. I slid right down that slippery slope and went tumbling.

I suppose I don't have to mention that no one clapped for me. When Kurumi-sensei indicated the next student in line should introduce themselves, the room was so silent you could hear a pin drop.

"It's all over. My quiet new life is all over! I was supposed to be popular and get lots of, um . . . *private* time with the girls."

"I don't know if private time with the girls is compatible with a quiet life, ryui."

What an obnoxious, vicious monster! The rest of the students all just simply said their names, what club they were in, and what school they had come from. I was the only one who'd acted weird!

Ugh! I set my chin down on my desk and sighed. I felt awful. It was like someone had yelled, "It's a race!" and I'd taken off running and cannonballed into a pool, only to turn around and see everyone else sitting around and relaxing.

Of course, none of them followed me. And of course, no one told me that it wasn't even pool day. The rest of them just held hands and ran the race, acting like the best of friends.

I had no other recourse. I just sat there and vaguely listened to the other students introduce themselves. As I listened to them talk, it became clear that the vast majority of them had come from Mikagura Middle School. There were only a few students who, like myself, had applied to Mikagura Academy from an unrelated school system. To make matters worse, even though the school was unbelievably large, everyone seemed to know each other because of the club battle system.

Even those students that weren't representatives of their clubs still seemed to know everyone through other opportunities and club requirements, like practices and socials.

It was starting to sink in—I was really out of my league.

Even the new students, who had just arrived yesterday, had mostly already chosen and joined clubs. I was starting to get worried.

Could it be? Could I be the only idiot in the school who still hadn't joined a club? Weren't there any other kids forced to live in sleeping bags?

Sigh . . .

"I guess I better get moving."

I need to join a club and start making friends as soon as possible. Because of my introduction debacle, I felt like I'd fallen pretty low in the eyes of my new classmates. I had to reverse course soon and get them all on my side.

I decided to go around and visit as many clubs as I could, once classes were finished for the day.

It was time to get out of that sleeping bag and get out of my self-imposed social isolation.

Listening to the rest of my classmates introduce themselves, I realized that there were actually far more clubs available than had been featured in the welcome party. If there were a lot of options, I was sure to find somewhere I'd fit in!

Sure, I had to hurry. But I didn't want to rush and just choose something at random either. After all, that wouldn't be much fun, would it?

The academy was a very strange place, but the classes themselves were just like anywhere else. If I really had to point out the differences, they were simple enough.

The devices we'd been assigned upon acceptance were frequently incorporated into the lessons and the points we earned through the battle system also ended up being used in our academic classes in various ways. You could spend your points to be excused from different subjects. And you could even use them to see hints during your tests!

The battle system points really did seem to influence every aspect of life on campus.

My first day at the academy was a wild rollercoaster ride. But I finally made it to the end of classes.

"Whew! Everyone else seems to understand how everything works, but I feel totally clueless!" I stretched and ate alone. Bimii copied me, imitating the way I stretched. It annoyed me, so I slapped him.

"Ouch! What was that for, ryui!?"

"I'll ask the questions here! What was with that introduction your wrote for me? It was so confusing. It made me look like an idiot!"

I felt like I was the only one that didn't fit in with the rest of the class. I wasn't going to pretend like Bimii's speech hadn't had something to do with that. It's not like they were treating me differently just because I'd come from another school.

Sleeping Bag-chan—I mean Katai-chan—was the only one that even looked in my direction, but she was too busy with her new circle of friends to spend her time checking on me.

I had always been the mood-maker, the girl surrounded by a gaggle of friends. This situation was almost too much for me to bear! For the first time in a long time, I was all alone, casting questioning looks all around the building. It was still too early for me to leave the lecture hall. Just when I was wondering what I should do . . .

"Eruna-chan! Sorry to keep you waiting, but I'm finally here! Here it is: my dramatic, splendid entry!"

My cousin, Shigure, came walking over, calling out with a fake sense of ease. I'd basically forgotten that he existed, so I certainly hadn't been waiting for him. But he acted as if it were the most obvious thing in the world, so without thinking, I slipped into behaving as if I had been. "Uh-huh. You're late."

When he entered the lecture hall, the whole room seemed to suddenly grow quiet. People seemed to be holding their breath.

Was it because he was an upperclassman? Was it so rare for an upperclassman to visit the freshman classrooms?

I felt the eyes of the room on me again, and people were whispering to each other. I felt it even more than I had during my introduction speech. I wasn't imagining it—I couldn't be!

"Hey, isn't that Shigure-san? Of the Manga Club's *Hero Time*?"

"I think so! I've seen him in the school newspaper before! I can't believe he's actually here! Why would such a famous person come visit our class?"

"Maybe he has to talk with the new teacher or something like that? He's sitting next to Ichinomiya. You don't think he knows that trickster, do you?"

"Ahaha, you mean Eruna-san? Of course he doesn't know her! I mean, she's from a different school system!"

They were definitely talking about me. I couldn't hear everything they were saying, but I was sure it was about me. I have very refined intuition for these things. I could smell it.

Because I had learned how the battle system was really important, I was better equipped to understand what was going on. The club representatives must have occupied extremely influential positions. Everyone must have looked up to them.

It sounded like the middle school students followed the high school battles regularly through videos and the newspapers. This meant that some of these new students had probably only seen Shigure on TV. I guess it wasn't so strange that they would react so dramatically to seeing him in person. Thinking back on it, Asuhi-kun had also been pretty impressed to meet Shigure the day before. As I saw it, Shigure was just a weirdo with an unhealthy amount of affection for his cousin.

"Shigure, you didn't explain things well enough! Why didn't you tell me yesterday how important it was for me to join a club!?"

"S . . . Sorry. I thought that Bimii-san had told you all about it."

Bimii-*san*!? I guess he was technically an instructor, so I guess it made sense to be polite. I'd been pretty rude to him from the moment we met, so it felt kind of crazy to hear him treated so politely.

I mean, if a mosquito came buzzing into your room, wouldn't it feel strange to bow and call it mosquito-san?

"Eruna, you're the sort of person that can only take in so much information at once, ryui. I was just trying to be organized and teach you things when you were ready for them, ryui."

"How rude! Are you calling me stupid? I'm like a sponge! A big, sopping wet sponge! I can learn anything!"

Bimii just nodded along while I complained. He didn't seem very concerned. I guess he had a point though. Whenever I stayed up late cramming for a test, I could never remember most of what I read. And whenever I went overcapacity, I would start forgetting things in the order that I'd reviewed them. I forgot the older stuff to make room for the new stuff. It was a miserable cycle.

It was regrettable, but I had to admit that there might have been a shred of truth in Bimii's judgment.

"Most of the clubs offer a trial period for admission. Why don't you try a few of them out today?"

Shigure smiled and tried to cheer me up.

No matter how ferociously I attacked him, Shigure never struck back. He was always just my kind, warm cousin.

"Trial periods, eh? I really just want to join one, so that I can have a room to sleep in."

I understood the need to take your time when making a big decision like that, but was I supposed to sleep in the hallway the whole time I was thinking? I can't really describe how powerless and lonely it felt to be relegated to a sleeping bag.

"Then why don't you try joining the Manga Research Club? You'd fit right in!"

"I would rather die! Just thinking about it gives me creeps. You'll just make me the model for some over-the-top, personal manga fantasy of yours! The last thing I need is you ogling more than you already do!"

I didn't want to sacrifice my happiness that easily. I wasn't going to sell my soul so quickly. If I had to get by on small meals and sleep in the hallway, well, so be it! At least I could respect myself.

Shigure just stood there looking confused about why I was so insistent. Fine. He didn't have to understand. I wasn't going to change my mind.

"I'll never, NEVER join the Manga Research Club!"

My classmates were still watching me with fascination when I went running from the room. I could let them start talking. I didn't want to get a reputation for hanging out with Shigure, not if I could help it.

There were plenty of times in the past, like when I first started going to middle school, when I hadn't been careful enough guarding my relationship with Shigure from others, leading to some unnecessary misunderstandings. I certainly didn't understand where they were coming from, but it sure seemed Shigure was pretty popular with the other girls. If I kept hanging out with him, then I'd have to deal with the jealously of my other classmates, like I'd been forced to do once or twice in the past. But I'd grown up since then! I wasn't going to make the same mistake twice!

"Wait for me, ryui! Don't leave me, ryui!"

Bimii, startled by my sudden departure, took off flying after me. He carried my bag in his mouth. It actually looked like it was a little too heavy for him to handle. I guess he was stronger than he looked. I had to admit that, for the first time, he looked a little cute.

I looked back and Shigure just shrugged disappointedly. He didn't look like he was going to follow me.

At the very least, he had figured out not to take

things too far. He always pushed me up to the point I could handle and then stopped. It was hard to tell how sincere he was about the things he was always saying. It was really too bad. It was like I had him in the palm of my hand—how boring!

I left the lecture hall and ran down the hallway, but then . . .

"What the heck!?" I shouted and skidded to a stop before a bulletin board.

It was so tall that I couldn't reach the top of it. It spread out for a few meters on each side. Despite being so large, it was completely covered with posters and bulletins. There wasn't a spare inch of the thing that wasn't covered in a layer or two. They all seemed to be notices from the various clubs.

"Whoa! Now that's really something! I never knew there were so many different kinds of culture-themed clubs!"

"No matter how minor the activity, you can form a club as long you have three people who want to be members, ryui! So there are a lot of small clubs. There are clubs that get really popular and large because of their performance in the battles, ryui!"

You only needed three people? It was much easier to form a club at Mikagura than it would be at a normal school. That meant I only needed two friends to form my own club. That sounded pretty interesting to me, but then again, I didn't think there were any other students who hadn't yet joined a club yet. So there was no one left for me to invite and I didn't have any ideas for a club, anyway.

"By the way, ever since Shigure became the representative of the Manga Research Club, he's done exceptionally well in the battles, which has made him very popular, ryui!"

"I don't believe it! You mean Shigure is that impressive!? Whatever! I'll never join his club!"

"You make me curious about what he did to earn all this hate from you, ryui."

That would take a while to explain, if I bothered to explain it.

Looking over all the flyers, I couldn't help but be entertained by the sheer originality of them all. I felt like I could stand there staring at them all day.

"I guess I'll start trying out some clubs, starting with

the ones I saw at the welcome party and then moving on to other clubs that look interesting. It might end up taking a little time, but I want to choose a club where I'll really fit in."

"Good idea, ryui. Once you join a club, it's not easy to switch to a different one, so you better make sure you know where you want to be. Let's go, ryui!"

Well, that made it clear as day. The only place to start would be the club that *she* was in. Why pick a club based on its subject matter when you could pick based on who's in it? Right?

"Okay, Bimii, take me to the goddess's club!"

*

I relaxed my shoulders, knelt, and started to grind my bar of ink on the inkstone. The Calligraphy Club was housed in a large Japanese-style room and the air was filled with the smell of new tatami mats and the earthy smell of fresh ink. But I was not in the mood to enjoy it. I was too busy being heartbroken.

Almost as if to deny my feelings, the other club members were all chatting and joking so loudly that it felt like they were trying to undue hundreds of years of calligraphy's image. Wasn't it something you did in solemnity and silence? Most of the students were not doing calligraphy at all. They were just sitting around chatting with their friends.

I'd expected to see everyone dressed in hakama, but everyone seemed to just be dressed in whatever they liked. I felt betrayed. Where was the stuffy, old, oppressive space that I'd been expecting?

"Seisa-san turned you down, so you came to check out the Calligraphy Club? I'm fine with that, but I doubt you've improved much since I saw you yesterday," said Himi-chan.

Right, that's right. I went to go try out the goddess's club, but when I got there, she just turned me away and said they weren't looking for new members at the moment.

I didn't know that they were allowed to do that, so it had come as quite a shock. I was a little depressed over it, actually. I'd really been looking forward to my after school adventures with the goddess. But! But . . . "Seisa-senpai's club is the 'Going Home' Club? Can you believe that? Does that really count as a culture-themed activity? Doesn't it sound like it should be against the rules?"

"She's the granddaughter of the academy headmaster, ryui. She was permitted to form a unique club like that in exchange for agreeing to be the model in the pamphlet, ryui."

Bimii perched on my shoulder and tried to calm me down. The idea of a Going Home club wouldn't have even occurred to me.

I pursed my lips and leaned my weight down on the inkstone. After my horrible rejection, I went wandering near the Calligraphy Club, crestfallen and confused. When Katai-chan passed by, she invited me to come check the club out. Speaking of Katai-chan . . .

"Katai-chan! You have such great intuition for this! I can't believe you're really just a beginner. You're doing so well!"

"Ehehe . . . You . . . You really think so?"

She seemed to be getting along really well with the other girls in the club. She was wearing an assigned hakama, and I couldn't help but notice that it didn't really fit her quite right. It was a little puffy and loose in places. She looked great!

I'd be spending the night alone in my sleeping bag, while she'd be surrounded by the warm embrace of her hakama-wearing club friends! Can you believe it? Who would think that handwriting would have such a dramatic effect on our lives?

I know that Katai-chan was only trying to be nice when she reached out to me. We'd both been stuck in those sleeping bags, but she had moved onwards and upwards before I could. She'd reached out to me, even though she didn't have to. It's not like we'd known each other very well at all before that, so I could tell she was a nice girl.

The devil that sleeps in me, Devil Eruna—no, wait . . . *Deruna* (just thought it up, but it's better to shorten things to make them catchy, right?) wouldn't be satisfied so easily. She was busy whispering in my ear, "Katai-chan thinks you look like a pet hamster she used to have, devil. That's why she's being nice to you, devil!"

"Shut up, Devil Eruna! (The shortened version didn't really have the impact I think a nickname needs for longevity, so I retired it.) Stop playing mind games with me! And your catchphrase is a little too on-the-nose to be clever! Have you no shame!?"

"Not at all, devil! I'm sticking with it, devil! Katai-chan thinks you look just like her old hamster, Beetle Back (female), and that's why she's being nice to you, devil!"

"She named her hamster 'Beetle Back (female)'? She has terrible taste in names! Is it necessary to include 'female' in the name? Poor little Beetle Back must have been so stressed out over that name. That's probably why it ran on its wheel all night long! The poor thing was just trying to run from its name!"

What did Devil Eruna mean? Did I look like a hamster? As far as I know, I'm a human. Just how many hamster-like qualities did I have?

There was only one way to rid myself of the doubts that plagued me. I'd have to ask her directly. But how was I supposed to bring that up and make it look casual? I couldn't just broach the subject without some kind of introduction. I ran over possibilities in my mind, but before I could come up with anything good, Katai-chan broke the silence.

"Beetle . . . I mean, Ichinomiya-san, are you having any trouble with that ink?"

"Hey now! You just called me Beetle Back, didn't

you!? I guess I don't have to figure out a way to ask you about it. You obviously have me confused with your hamster, don't you!?"

"Oh no . . . not at all! Um . . . Are you hungry? Do you want some sunflower seeds?"

"Ha! You think you can tempt me with seeds!? Aren't you even going to try and hide the way you feel? You're just going to run with it, aren't you? Well, I'll have you know that I'm not a hamster! I'm a human being!"

"I know that. You don't have to yell at me. I know! Beetle Back went to live in the sky a long time ago. He's . . . he's not a part of this world anymore," she sniffed. "Waaaah!"

"You're kind of making ME look like the bad guy here. You're making it look like I said something mean to you! Can you stop crying and holding those sunflower seeds out to me now!? What do I have to do!? Are you going to force me to eat those things!?"

I didn't see any way out of it. I pounced on the seeds and started to chew them. Devil Eruna looked on with an evil grin plastered across her face, while I tried to console Katai-chan. What was going on? Was I stuck in a nightmare?

"Ichinomiya-san? Ichinomiya-san?"

Someone was shaking me awake. Oh no! Grinding the ink was so boring and repetitive that I'd started to fall asleep.

I'd just had the strangest terrifying dream. Oh well, I'd have to forget it. I'd have to forget it and move on. Full speed ahead! I guess I hadn't gotten the best night of sleep in the hallway.

"Oh, hello, Katai-chan. Thanks, but I don't want any sunflower seeds."

"Um . . . that's good?"

I'd made up my mind to forget it all. The lingering images from the dream spoke to its power. I remembered the end of it now. I'd pounced on the seeds and chewed them up. In the dream, she'd really made me chow down on a lot of them.

Katai-chan turned her head to the side and seemed to be confused. I wished she would stop looking at me that way! Stop it! She looked at me just like she would look at Beetle Back!

"Eruna-chan, I think you should give up on the Calligraphy Club for now. I can see that you're troubled by it, and of course, I'd love to just let you in, but . . ."

"That's true. I had problems the last time. And I just sat down to write something and fell asleep in the middle of it."

Himi-chan was trying to turn me down in the nicest, most euphemistic way she could. It was nice of her to give me another chance, but she might have been right. Maybe I just wasn't cut out for the Calligraphy Club.

In the end, I ended up leaving without trying to convince them any further. I just thanked them for their time and left the room.

"You can always talk to me, okay? Come by any time!" Himi-chan shouted with a smile, as if there was nothing wrong in the world. Katai-chan stood next to her, nodding her agreement but also looking a little troubled.

I could tell that they both wanted to help me. I had made things harder on myself than I needed to, but there were people to help me. Not just Shigure and Bimii, but now Katai-chan and Himi-chan, too! My circle of friends was growing slowly but surely.

"Thanks! I'll swing by the next time I'm feeling sleepy!" I tried to hide my embarrassment with a joke. I think they understood what I meant, because they both smiled and waved to me as I left.

I went up to the stairway that led to the roof, thinking that I could calm down a bit if I had some fresh air.

The sun had fallen down below the trees and the campus was slipping into twilight.

Maybe it was because the campus was surrounded by so much greenery, or maybe it was just the time of day, but I felt like the air was purifying me from within as I filled my lungs. It felt different than breathing the air back home.

I climbed the stairs to the roof and pulled on the door at the top. It wasn't locked and swung open easily.

"Wow! Look at that! I feel like I can reach out and touch the stars! It's amazing!"

The rooftop felt like a completely different world. The campus didn't have any tall buildings on it. So if you looked up from the roof, there was nothing to block your view of the sparkling sky. It was beautiful.

We were deep in the mountains, too. So there wasn't any light to make it hard to see the stars. Each one stood out bright and distinct, like a planetarium.

"It surprised me the first time, too, ryui. Because the academy is in such a picturesque and dark environment, the Astronomy Club has become very popular, ryui!"

"Really? Well, if the stars are this beautiful, of course people would want to look at them. They look good without a telescope, so I can only imagine what it would be like with one!"

I felt like dragging my sleeping bag up to the roof so that I could sleep under the stars. I surprised even myself—who knew that I had such a sentimental side? I felt like laughing.

Eventually, I lowered my gaze back to the rooftop. The school building was very large, so the roof itself seemed to stretch out indefinitely in every direction. It almost felt like a waste that no one else was up there enjoying the view.

"Do you think that person over there is in the Astronomy Club? They seem to be looking through a telescope!"

There actually was one person there, very far away from the door I'd come through. It looked like a short boy leaning over a telescope.

I'd been ooh-ing and ahh-ing and making plenty of noise while I looked up at the unbelievable sky, but it looked like all my gasping hadn't bothered the boy. He didn't seem to have noticed my presence.

"What a good opportunity, ryui! Why don't you go ask him if you can try out the club, ryui!?"

"Hey, that's a good point! That might be the best idea you've ever had, Bimii. You're finally being useful!"

"Really? You think THAT was a personal best for me, ryui? What does that say about my life up until now, ryui?"

He hadn't taken it as a joke and he fell into deep thought. I thought of a number of snappy comebacks, but he looked pretty serious, so I decided to hold back for once.

I walked steadily through the dark toward the boy. When I got close enough, I realized that I recognized him by his style and the unmistakable color of his hair.

"Heeey! Isn't that Asuhi-kun I see over there?"

It was Asuhi Imizu, the boy I met at the welcome party, who had come from Mikagura Middle School and was in the Astronomy Club. He finally noticed me when I called out to him, and he smiled when he realized it was me.

"Eruna-san! So you've already come to see the stars? I was hoping you'd stop by!"

I remembered him inviting me to look at the stars

back at the party. I hadn't intended to go looking for him, but I was glad that I ran into him on the roof.

His cheeks blushed and his eyes seemed to look everywhere but at me. I tried to catch his eyes to see what he was thinking, but he kept avoiding my gaze. It was kind of cute. Was he really a boy? Everything he did looked so . . . feminine!

I actually think he was more girly than I was, but it would probably hurt his feelings if I told him that.

"Asuhi-kun, are you alone up here? Did the other club members already head home?"

He shook his head. "The upperclassmen aren't here yet! But this was my first chance to make some observations at the school. I just couldn't wait any longer, so I came up here by myself."

He spoke very quickly, looking embarrassed. He had that in common with Himi-chan. He had that sort of small animal quality. The thought of it made me picture a hamster, which brought back the rough memories from the Calligraphy Club. No! I had to let it go. Farewell, Beetle Back.

I didn't want to scare him off, and I didn't want him to distrust me, so I took a few deep breaths before

continuing the conversation. It didn't occur to me that it might look strange for a girl to run over to someone, out of the dark, and stand there, breathing.

"Oh yeah? Neat! Hey, can I take a peek through that thing? If the sky is this pretty to the naked eye, I can only imagine what it must look like through a real telescope! Does it make the stars look like they are right there in front of you? Like they are closer than the convenience store? Like they are only 30 paces away? Hm?"

"You went a little overboard there, ryui. How can you look at the gorgeous night sky and think about it like it's a 24-hour store that you can pop into for a Chinese bun, ryui?"

What was the problem? Was I not allowed to think about the stars however I wanted? Were they so special? Who was Bimii to give me orders? Was he a CEO? Did he think I was his secretary? Did he think I worked for him!?

Granted, I might have imagined CEOs different from they really were, but how was I supposed to know what they were really like?

"Wait just a second. I'll set it up for you," said Asuhi. He wasn't concerned with the endless string of questions I proposed and answered for myself—he seemed like he was just happy that someone had showed interest in the stars. He cheerfully fiddled with the telescope settings. He was such a pure, innocent thing. Could I be like him if I tried really hard?

If I did, there was no doubt in my mind that Shigure would think I was sick. He'd try to calm me down and bring me back to normal, even if he had to force me. What kind of person was I, in the end? Did I need a personality adjustment?

Asuhi was adjusting the angle and height of the telescope. He even pulled out a wet tissue to clean the eyepiece, even though it already looked very clean to me. If he was going to put this much effort into getting it ready, I had better be a good enough observer to make it worth it! I had never, not even once, looked through an astronomical telescope before.

Should I have dressed up for the occasion? What would have been appropriate? A bowtie? Should I have dressed up as a portly gentleman with a cane? What would a person like that use for a catchphrase? "I'll need the receipt, too?"

"Eruna, I hate to interrupt when I don't have to,

but I think you're really confused about how people dress for things, ryui. I don't think any occasion would require you to become a 'portly man,' ryui."

"Oh, hey! Whenever I think about gentlemen, I always model the character off of an uncle of mine."

"Then I think your uncle might be a *different* sort of gentleman, ryui," said Bimii, looking somehow sad.

So many of my beliefs had needed updates over the course of the day.

While Bimii and I debated the particulars, Asuhi finished setting up the telescope and stood aside, motioning to the seat before it.

"There! Go ahead and take a look! You won't be able to look away! Oh, and that button there is very dangerous. Please don't touch it."

"Thank you! I'm so excited! But why would there be a dangerous button on the side of a telescope? Can it zoom indefinitely?"

I was so ignorant about the machine that I couldn't even picture what could be dangerous about it. At the very least, I needed to make sure I didn't break it. When someone says "don't touch this," I have to wonder if it's some sort of trick. Maybe what they meant to say was, "please touch this." I had the soul of an entertainer, after all. But I decided it would be best to control my impulses for the time being. The telescope was so large that Asuhi could barely fit his arms around it, which made me suspect that it might be very expensive. I had to treat it like a gentleman would—no, wait!—how a *lady* would.

Quickly, but cautiously, I set my eye against the eyepiece and looked in. I didn't know what to expect, but when I saw the sky through the telescope I let out a shriek, "Ahhh!" I'd never heard my own voice sound like that.

"What? What is this? You're telling me this isn't CG? You're telling me this isn't from that new Last Fantasy game? What I'm seeing exists in the very same universe as myself?"

"Your impression of a *lady* is getting better, ryui. That last sentence was very refined, ryui."

I'd obviously never thought of myself as a lady, so I guess my impression wasn't spot-on. Whatever—this was no time to worry about something like that.

It was *absorbing—engrossing!* Those were the only words that fit. I couldn't believe I was seeing the same sky I had just looked at. There was so much light!

I could only whimper and sigh. I couldn't bring myself to look away.

"Heh, isn't it beautiful? I've been watching the stars since elementary school. They have so many different ways of appearing. I never get tired of looking at them."

Normally, I would have reacted with scorn to a phrase like that, but for the first time in my life, I found myself nodding along. He was right.

"I feel like I could look at them forever. If you get to look at this kind of thing every day, then the Astronomy Club sounds great."

"Well, some days are cloudy, so you don't get a view like this every day. But you're certainly welcome to join!"

He was blushing again, but I knew that he hadn't meant anything by it. I mean, I'd spoken with Shigure the same way at the welcome party. So if I sounded like I had feelings for Asuhi, that would mean I had feelings for Shigure, too—and that's just crazy.

Still, I was a little happy that he'd invited me. I felt myself starting to blush, too. Without removing my eye from the telescope, I fanned myself with a free hand.

"Watch out, Eruna-san! That's dangerous! You brushed the button!"

"Huh? What? The button? Oh, no!"

When I fanned myself without looking I'd been careless enough to touch the button he'd specifically warned me about.

It was soft and sunk down without offering any resistance. At the same time a piercing, splitting sound shrieked out from the telescope as a bazooka-like shot of stardust shot from the end with a powerful blast.

"It's dangerous, so please! Please step away from that weapon!"

"What? What is this? Did you just call it a weapon?"

Before he told me to move, I had already reflexively jumped back from the telescope.

That thing really WAS dangerous!

The shot of light it had made faded away pretty quickly, but I could still feel the heat it had produced radiating from the telescope.

"Oh, I'm sorry. I should have been more clear about the danger. This is a telescope, but it is also my battle cannon that I use for the club battles. I'm sorry to scare you like that."

Asuhi quickly apologized and tried to calm me down. So he attacked his opponents with that giant ball of starlight? That seemed pretty cool, but wasn't it too hot? Wasn't it too powerful?

Asuhi-kun was so soft-spoken and kind that it was very hard to picture him ever attacking anyone. It was a real shock to see that he used such a powerful weapon.

I'm sure that the battles were treated like a sport and there were strict rules governing the way attacks should be made, to make sure that no one got hurt, right?

"My ability is called 'shooting star.' My telescope collects starlight and then uses it to form an attack. As long as I get the telescope to collect the energy, anyone can launch the attack by pushing the button. That makes it a little hard to manage. But of course, the attack is much stronger if I'm the one to launch it."

Nearly all of the students at Mikagura eventually discovered that they had special battle abilities. The students that ended up being club representatives tended to have stronger attack abilities than the other students. At least that's what Bimii told me. It all made sense now. I really was living in a *fantasy world*. That explained why the academy had such a strange battle system in place.

"That was an impressive attack, ryui! I know you just started attending the academy, but if you have skills like that, you'll be the Astronomy Club representative in no time. You've really improved since middle school. I can see that you are brimming with potential, ryui!"

"Don't say that. I . . . I still have so far to go."

"I can't believe we are both first-year students here! I don't even know what club I'm joining and I certainly don't have any special abilities!"

Bimii must have kept a close eye on the students in middle school, which I guess meant that he took his job as instructor pretty seriously. And I thought he just flapped around, looking weird.

But eventually, I would have to join a club. That meant I would have to start using a weapon, too, right? When would I awaken to my abilities? Where was I headed? Where did I want to go? I didn't have answers to any of those questions.

The Astronomy Club certainly had potential, but was it something I wanted to stick with for years? I didn't think so. When I told Asuhi-kun, he flashed a disappointed smile and said, "Well, I guess that's that. You don't have to join the club, but I hope you'll come hang out and look at the stars with me from time to time. I hope you find what you want to do, Eruna-san."

"Yeah! And I promise not to touch the button again. So I hope you'll let me look through your telescope in the future!"

He shook my hand and walked me to the door. His hands were so soft—just like a girl's! But they were warm and steady, too.

He waved goodbye when I slipped through the door.

I had one month. There was a crazy rule that new students who hadn't chosen a club within one month were to be expelled. I could feel the pressure weighing on me.

I wanted to get back to the dorms and get some sleep, even though all that was waiting for me was a cold sleeping bag in the hallway. I had to live out in the open, with no privacy at all.

"I really want my own room! I want to sleep in a bed!"

My desperate pleas echoed in the stairwell. What clubs did I want to try out next? I knew that I was in a rush and that I had to join something soon—so why did I keep finding things to be dissatisfied with? There must have been a part of me that was more excited than uncomfortable. That alone was surprising.

*

"Hello all! It's me, Eruna Ichinomiya, and I'm the next big thing! I've come to try out the Drama Club! Since kindergarten, I've been entrusted with the most essential roles in school plays, like trees and bushes. I have the potential to become a famous actress—you wouldn't want to pass on me!"

It was after school on the following day. After getting a taste of the other clubs, I realized that I would have to be more proactive about finding a place to fit in. So this was my first attempt at that.

It didn't matter what club you were in, but you had to join a club if you went to Mikagura. Too much of your life there depended on it. I was surviving on little food and even my showers were cut down to under five minutes. I'm a GIRL! They wanted me to take four-minute showers!? The timer ran out when I had all the shampoo still in my hair and I had to rinse it all out with cold water. I felt like I was going to cry.

There was no getting around it. Everything required points and the only points I received were for attending classes. It was the lowest amount you could have. If I just joined a club, any club, I'd have way more points than I did now. And I'd finally be able to start living like a human again.

I ended up at the cafeteria with Katai-chan in the morning. She paid for my breakfast. She felt sympathy for me when I sat down in front of her with only an unflavored rice ball and a glass of tap water. She really was a nice girl.

I had to join a club soon, so I decided to try out the Drama Club. Based on the number of members, it was supposed to be one of the largest and most popular clubs at the school. But I'd gone to visit as soon as class got out, so there wasn't really anyone around when I got there.

The room was completely littered with props and costumes and set pieces. It was very chaotic. Oh hey, they even had the tree costume I'd once worn when I made my acting debut!

But something was weird. When I threw open the door and shouted my prepared greeting, the few students that were there didn't say anything back to me. They just sat there, staring at me with their mouths agape.

Himi-chan had told me that my introduction would be my chance to make an impression, so I'd tried to do the best that I could. The reaction wasn't what I'd been hoping for. Still, I felt like I'd really pulled something off with my dramatic entrance. I wonder what they didn't like about it?

"Oh, um . . . new girl? This isn't the nurse's office, you know? It's easy to overdo things in the springtime, I know, but just keep at it, okay? You'll make it!"

"Um, okay. Why are you treating me like a crazy person!? Was my introduction too over-the-top!?"

A senpai with the cat-eared hood on—pretty stylish if you ask me—talked down to me from the second I walked in. She looked like she was genuinely concerned though, which somehow made it even worse.

Just like I'd seen at the welcome party, the club members that were milling around the room had all altered their uniforms to make different animal motifs.

The girl senpai (I only assumed she was older than me because her chest was so large) was a cat. There was also a boy who looked like a rabbit and someone who looked like a pig, a bear, and so on. Nearly everyone was dressed like an animal.

The plain uniforms were plenty cute as they were, but this was really something. The club had rules for who was to play what animal. If I were to join the club, would they make me a hippopotamus? Or would they make me a sloth? It didn't matter what parts I was assigned in the plays, but if I had to walk around campus dressed like a hippopotamus, I was going to be pretty upset about it.

I was carefully observing the people in the room when I realized that the conversation had trailed off a while ago. Just when I thought maybe I should say something . . .

"This girl isn't crazy, ryui! Okay, well she might be a LITTLE crazy, but she stopped by to try out the club, ryui! You're right to think she's a little crazy, but she's just stopping by for the day, so I hope you'll show her a good time, ryui!"

Bimii stepped in and mediated our discussion, like

an instructor should. But it didn't really sound like he was sticking up for me, did it?

"Oooh! You're such a cute little instructor! Mu-wahhhh!"

"Urm, ugh! Pah! Let . . . Let me go, ryui!"

The girl with the cat ears had leapt at Bimii and hugged him tight against her chest. I kind of wished I could trade places with him. I didn't really have any points left on my device, but I'd use whatever I did have to buy him all the snacks he could eat—if only he would trade places with me!

It looked so soft and comfy that, before I realized it, I had started drooling. I wiped away the drool with the sleeve of my uniform and tried to focus.

And yet . . . they were so big and puffy that I could hardly believe it. They looked like they were straight out of a manga—like they might pop. It's a little hard to explain. Sorry about that.

"So what's the story? I'm supposed to make a pass at you, Eruna Ichinomiya-san?"

"I said you 'wouldn't want to pass on me!' What did think I was saying!?"

"Huh? So you're hardboiled?"

"Are you kidding me? You're doing this on purpose, and you're going to make me cry! It's like one of those dramas where, at the end of the story, I eat some food that my grandma used to make and the background music turns into some ballad from the '80s!"

"So you're being hunted or something?"

"You're still keeping this game going? I already said it: *you won't want to pass on me!* Stop looking at me with pity! Anyway, why would I be hunted? Do I look like an animal to you? Come on people!"

The club members all took turns making fun of me. What was going on? The cat girl still had a death grip on Bimii. He didn't look like he could breathe. Things were starting to get out of control!

Should I assume that the club members that were there didn't represent the behavior of the rest of the club? If the entire Drama Club acted this way then there was no way I could join up—they'd kill me! It would be a bad way to go: death by overplayed jokes. I could see it now. They'd report my passing on the evening news. I was too young to die!

I was wearing myself out just thinking about it. I sighed deeply and looked around the room for an escape route. In the back, surrounded by various set pieces, I spotted a large sofa. There was a boy lounging on it. When he saw me, he yawned dramatically and then flipped up off the sofa with an acrobatic flair.

"Did you just do a back flip off of the couch? What are you trying to prove? You can just stand up, you know?"

"What do you know? I just wanted to, um, stretch! Because I was lying down! You get it?"

A portion of his bangs fell lazily over one eye, which made me realize I was looking at Yuto Akama, the Drama Club representative. He hopped over to us, looking somewhat embarrassed.

He had a look in his eyes that made him seem like he was hiding something. He spoke just like you'd imagine a boy in his mid-teens would. He looked like he'd be pretty easy to get along with.

Just as his first impression had led me to believe, he seemed to be well-liked by the other club members. When he walked over in our direction, they all naturally formed a circle around him, making him the center of attention. It was clear from the way they all looked at him that they genuinely liked him, and that's why they surrounded him. And it wasn't just because he was the club representative.

"I think I heard the gist of the conversation from back there. However, we need to consider our prospective members carefully."

"Sounds good to me! Hey everyone, did you just hear what Akama-kun said? You have to take her seriously! Did you hear that? Akama-kun says take her seriously!"

"I didn't mean it that way, and you know it! Stop making that face, like you think you really said something smart!"

"Hmm . . . I think you DID mean it like that!"

Judging from the way Akama-kun reacted to their chiding, I got the feeling that the club liked to have fun with him, just the way they'd been playing with me before. He looked like he couldn't believe they had turned on him. He just sighed and seemed ready to resign himself to the sort of treatment he'd dealt with in the past.

"Well, considering that you didn't stop by here on your first day, I guess it's safe to assume that the Drama Club wasn't your first choice, right? Where did you go before you came here?"

"Um . . . I tried out the Calligraphy and Astronomy Clubs! Both of them had been kind enough to offer me invitations, so I thought I'd check it out and see what the fuss was about!"

"That's not how it looked to me, ryui."

"The Astronomy Club? That's where Asuhi Imizu went," Akama-kun said softly, barely whispering. For a split second a dark expression flashed over his face. Then he blinked it away and acted like nothing had happened. He smiled. "Oh well. So you're here to try out the Drama Club, are you? I'll let you know up front that we don't really ask you to show off your acting chops right away. There are plenty of backstage jobs to choose from. Most of our members don't get to move into more prominent roles for a while. Everyone starts in support roles."

I sort of wanted the chance to show of my acting chops though—I'd really impressed everyone with my interpretation of a tree back in kindergarten. I thought about pushing for a chance to show off but decided against it, because I realized that it would also give them an opportunity to turn me away if they didn't like my work. I decided to just listen to what they had to say.

"And what do you want to do, Ichinomiya-chan? Did you have a particular role in mind? It doesn't have to be specific. If you want to work on acting or lighting or something, let us know."

What did I want to do? Honestly, I hadn't given it very much thought. If I was going to join the Drama Club, then I'd probably want to be acting on stage. I closed my eyes and tried to picture it.

It was just us girls on stage. We were all wearing flowing dresses. In fact, every single one of us was a princess. I guess in that situation I would dress like a boy and play the role of the prince. Preferably, the script would feature my character prominently. And it would include a lot of adult material. I'd heard of actors and actresses that completely immersed themselves in their roles, blurring the lines between their character and themselves. Just imagine what kind of trouble I could get myself into! There were so many possibilities. The boy club members would take all of the backstage work, but Akama-kun would get a special role. He could clean the toilet of the prince's house (three bedrooms!). Was I a little plump? I wasn't fat, but my long lazy vacation certainly hadn't helped my figure.

I nodded to myself and slowly opened my eyes to find Akama-kun standing nearby, looking at me with sympathy in his eyes. He was smiling though, which kind of freaked me out.

And he was way too close to me. Way too close!

"You said all of that out loud, you know? Unfortunately, I don't know if the Drama Club will be able to satisfy your ambitions. Or should I say your desires? And I'm not sure I could really pull off the role of a toilet cleaner."

"What!?"

"Right, right. Well hey, how about this? I've got a role that would be great for you! It's the turn-on-your-heels-and-head-straight-home type of character. I wonder if you can pull it off? Let's see! Bye-bye!"

And the whole club teamed up to push me out the door before I could even blink. All I'd managed to do was introduce myself. And that had been enough for them to turn me down!? They wouldn't even do me the favor of thinking about it for a little while? Was this sort of behavior normal? Couldn't they have even given some thought to the project I'd come up with for them?

It hadn't felt like a personal rejection. I didn't get

the impression that they were trying to be mean. But I also knew that it was one of the larger clubs, so maybe they just had to be careful about who they considered allowing in.

"Well, that gives us time to stop by one more place, doesn't it, Bimii? One more!"

"Are you drunk!? You sound like you're stumbling from bar to bar, ryui!"

I hadn't eaten any lunch that day, so if I was stumbling around, it was only because I was so hungry. I didn't want to explain that to him though, because it would only make me look more pathetic.

"Hey, I just had a GREAT idea! If this were a manga, you would have seen a light bulb flicker on over my head! If this were an RPG, I would have learned a new skill! It would play that little trumpet fanfare! You know, I think I might actually be a genius! Alright, full speed ahead! One more!"

"I have a feeling I'm not going to like this, ryui. Your 'good ideas' always make me worry, ryui."

"Hello, everyone! It's me, the newest student who LOVES flowers! When it's time for cherry blossom viewing, I spend more time focusing on my lunch! My head is full of fields of flowers, and I'm the talk of the town—it's me, Eruna Ichinomiya, and I'm here to check out the Flower Arranging Club! I hear you might have some really tasty ones around, so I'm ready to chow down. Show me the way!"

"That was terrible, ryui."

When I was pushed out of the Drama Club I didn't miss a beat—I ran straight for the Flower Arranging Club. For whatever reason (it's a mystery even to me) I always thought of flowers as if they were food. Actually, I'd seen it before on TV. There was a cooking show that had featured different kinds of flowers treated like tempura and they looked delicious. I couldn't get the image out of my mind. I was pretty hungry at that point, so I ran to the Flower -Arranging Club to see if I couldn't 'get a taste' of what they did there—if you know what I mean.

I'd shouted my arrival at the top of my lungs, but there was no sign that any one inside the room had heard me. It looked like there might not have been anyone there at all. It was a large Japanese-style room that ran alongside a hallway. The wall that lined the hallway was mostly glass so that people passing by could look inside at all the different arrangements that were on display.

I'm sure some of the pieces on display had been done by the teacher. But most of them were so beautiful I couldn't believe they'd been done by anyone even close to my age. I didn't know the first thing about flower arrangement, but I felt like I could stand there admiring them for a long time. It made me want to pretend I was an art critic visiting a gallery.

"Well, well. If it represents any school in particular, I'd say it comes from the one-eyed school. Yes, you can feel the aggressiveness in the arrangement."

"Masamune? Are you talking about Masamune? You know that one-eye refers to a dragon and not a school, right? And I don't know what you mean by 'aggressiveness.'"

It felt good just to imagine myself saying such sophisticated things. Of course, I didn't know anything about different schools or their founders. Weren't there days when you just want to pinch your chin and say something like, "I can see that the artist has the knowledge he needs, but is he capable of expressing it in form?" I want to do that maybe 50 times a year. Well, maybe not quite that much—that would put it at once a week. Anyway, this was one of those days, regardless. Yup.

"That one over there is in the Minatogawa style. And the one next to it is, too. Actually, all these arrangements are my own."

"Ahh! You scared me!"

Right behind me, a voice suddenly cut through the silence. I turned to find a boy in a kimono kneeling on a giant flower—he used it as if it were a cushion.

He cocked his head to the side, as if he couldn't figure out why I was acting so surprised. He definitely didn't feel like he had to hurry around for anyone except for himself.

Oh, I remembered that Bimii had told me about this boy back at the welcome party. He was the representative of the Flower Arranging Club, Sadamatsu Minatogawa! He was alone the last time I saw him, and he seemed to be alone now, too.

I looked quickly around the room and didn't see anyone, so maybe he was the only club member. There were plenty of flowers, but no other people.

Thinking he was going to continue the conversation,

I waited to see what he would say. But he didn't say anything at all. He just kept looking at me in silence. I'd never seen anyone so low-key in my life. He was like my mirror opposite! I never stopped talking, ever!

"All of these are your creations, Minatogawa-senpai? Where are the other members' pieces? Is there another room?"

I pointed through the wall of glass at the entrance and motioned to the back, where the room might have continued. Minatogawa-senpai just slowly shook his head. I thought he was going to explain further, but he didn't. He just sunk deeper into his flower cushion and started to pet its petals as if it were a pet.

I knew from the welcome party that this guy had the ability to make flowers bloom and to control them. So I wasn't so surprised when he held out his hand and a small flower suddenly appeared in it. To anyone else, the scene would have looked so bizarre as to be unbelievable. But it already felt normal to me. Was I the most adaptive person ever?

"The membership of the Flower Arranging Club has dropped every year. The people still in it don't seem very interested at all. It's just a ghost of its former self, ryui.

Now the club headquarters only feature Minatogawa-kun's work, ryui," Bimii whispered in my ear.

So that's what was going on. I felt bad running over to the club expecting an all-you-can- eat flower buffet. It wasn't looking like that was going to be an option. I had been hoping for a back and forth with the club members. "Let me join your club, so I can eat my fill of flowers!" "How could you say that? How terrible!" Yeah, a little fight like that would have been fun, but I wasn't going to get one. I had to give up. It was time to admit that flowers were not for eating.

I had never thought that flower arranging would be super popular with high school students in this day and age, but then again, I never thought that people hated it either.

"Minatogawa-kun, this is Eruna Ichinomiya, a new student here. She's come to try out the club, ryui!"

"Really? Do you . . . like flowers?"

When he heard that I wanted to try out the club, his face, just for a second, changed. He looked . . . happy.

Things could have gone badly, but luckily enough, he didn't seem to have heard my boisterous introduction. He probably would have been sad to hear how much I

wanted to chow down on his flowers. If the club was as low on members as Bimii had suggested, then he was probably pretty desperate to get new people to apply. So of course, he would have been sad to hear that his only applicant was only into flowers because she was hungry.

I admit it—I had only come to the club on a momentary whim, but meeting Minatogawa-senpai there and seeing his beautiful arrangements, and breathing in the floral air, made me think that I really might want to join. For my whole life, I'd been like that undisciplined dog in the neighborhood who barks all night or like the windshield wipers on a car that just keep going back and forth really quickly. People had always made fun of me for my excessive manic energy. It made me want to learn something refined and feminine. *Gimme that girl power!* Wouldn't flower arranging help with that? Wouldn't I be the pinnacle of refinement?

"To tell you the truth, I don't really know very much about flowers or about composition. But I'm really interested to learn about them!"

I made sure not to mention that I only thought of

them as a meal, because that definitely wasn't what he wanted to hear. I didn't want it to sound like I was lying to him either.

"You don't have to know anything. I'll teach you. I'd be glad if you discovered an interest in flowers."

He spoke slowly and calmly. I felt like I was being wrapped in the warmth of his voice. I was so happy that someone was finally welcoming me! If he personally taught me about it all, then I felt like I'd have no trouble learning. Could it be? Was I a fit for the Flower Arranging Club?

"I'd love to try! Let's do it!" I was getting excited, but Bimii didn't seem to agree. He was thinking about something silently. The poor thing really wasn't very good at judging the mood in a room, was he? He wasn't very good at feeling—or thinking! I don't think he even knew how to read! (Did I take that last part too far?)

Minatogawa-senpai noticed Bimii thinking, too, so we both just stood there, waiting to see what he was going to say.

"Eruna, do you know how to kneel properly for the arranging, ryui? Can you hold the seiza* position for very long? I know that Minatogawa-kun developed a style of arrangement that is done entirely from the seiza position, ryui. If your legs tend to fall asleep very quickly, then maybe you should look for another club."

What was he talking about? I'd seen pictures of arrangements being done while people stood or while they sat in chairs. Why would anyone invent a style that required you to kneel while you did it? Why?

I imagined that most of these things had been decided long ago and the clubs had to maintain the traditions—or something like that. If that were true, then they wouldn't want to make an exception for me.

Seiza. Hm . . . Seiza . . . I hate doing it, and I couldn't remember a time that I had to do it for very long. It made me wonder if I really could do it at all.

"You don't have to kneel the whole time. If you can hold the position for 30 minutes or so, you'll be okay."

Minatogawa-senpai offered an explanation without any prompting, which made me think that the seiza stuff must have turned off prospective club members in the past. I was starting to break into a cold sweat. I had a very bad feeling about what was coming next. Stop the bus! Get out of here, bad ending!

"Why don't you . . . just . . . try it out first, ryui? Just to make sure, ryui! I'm sure I'm just worrying for no good reason, but isn't it worth it just to check, ryui?"

"Um . . . yeah. Right. We'll just get that out of the way and move on to the real test, right? Okay! Let's go!"

"My leeeeeegs! Oh, my leeeeeegs!"

I had only been kneeling for one minute when my legs started to wobble and shake and go numb. Soon they started to feel like they'd been electrocuted. It had only been one minute! I thought I could make it longer than that! And Bimii was just flapping away, watching me. Stop it! If you want to laugh at me, laugh at me! If you want to lecture me, lecture me! Just stop staring at me!

I was too scared to even look at how Minatogawa-senpai was reacting. I couldn't look at him, but from what I could see, when I collapsed and rolled on the floor, he had buried his face in his hands and was looking pretty depressed. Things weren't looking good. They weren't looking good at all!

"Minatogawa-kun, I . . . I'm very sorry that I didn't stop Eruna from coming here today. I feel so guilty, ryui."

Good, he should feel guilty! What an ugly little monster! He was the one that showed me the way! I couldn't say anything like that though. I could hear the room freeze over. Fine, I didn't have to listen to anyone's lectures. I'd gotten the experience points I came for. I just kept rolling on the floor, waiting for my pins and needles to go away, and biting my lip out of shame.

"Too bad. I really would like to invite you to join the club, but it looks like you would have a very hard time with it. If only there were another club that taught a different style, you might have been a fit for a place like that."

A leaden, heavy feeling hung in the air. Whose fault was this!? Fine, I admit it. It was mine. The senpai looked very disappointed. I'd have to think of some way to cheer him up. But Bimii flew down and tackled me in the face, probably to keep me from making a further fool out of myself. I wanted to ask him if he couldn't think of a more peaceful way to do that, but I didn't want to dig myself a deeper hole. When I calmed down, I realized that he wasn't trying to tackle me, but comfort me. It still felt like he was punching me though.

"I'll come again when I learn how to kneel," I said,

and slowly trudged out of the room. It was a very large world out there, but I bet I'm the only girl that ever had her dreams crushed to dust because she wasn't good at kneeling!

I was starting to worry—really worry—that there might not be a club for me at the academy.

Little did I know that my fears would soon become reality.

*

"If you don't hurry up and decide soon, you're going to run out of time, ryui! You don't have the luxury of time to make this decision, ryui!"

He was right. It had already been three weeks since I started attending the academy, and I wasn't any closer to finding a club that I could join. You might say I was a freelancer of sorts.

The "free" part of that made it sound like I could savor my personal freedom. But the truth was that it meant I didn't have a job. It meant I was a NEET. It meant that no one wanted me in their organization!

I tried looking into the Art Club, too, but the

representative, Kuzuryu-senpai, turned me away at the door. He must have still been upset about our confrontation at the welcome party. I visited a new club every day but was always told that I wasn't suited to what they did or that they simply weren't recruiting new members.

Even worse, my reputation had already spread throughout the student body, because a lot of clubs started hiding their recruitment posters whenever I walked by.

What had I done to deserve all of this? I mean, sure—I DID sit out in front of the cafeteria with a sign that said, "Please give me some points, I'm hungry." And sure—I DID occasionally kick other people out of the showers so that I could have a couple more seconds of hot water. People had started calling me "the shower thief," which had a really sad ring to it, if you ask me. They eventually shortened it to just "thief," and when people showered in the evenings, they would scare each other by yelling, "The thief is coming!" Some of them would scream in fear, "Call the police! I'm scared!"

They did this whenever I walked down the hallway. In their eyes, I was the neighborhood pervert.

Still, I really should have joined a club by then. My new life was turning into a long chain of failures. I had to find a way to break it! I was only one week away from becoming subject to that dreaded rule: students that haven't joined a club within one month of enrollment were subject to expulsion.

It wasn't like I was being particularly picky, either. Not at all. I'd even thrown my pride in the trashcan and gone to check out Shigure's Manga Research Club.

Shigure had greeted me with open arms, literally crying with joy. But the other girls in the club shot daggers at me with their eyes, obviously afraid I was going to move in on their target. In the interest of my own safety, I had to leave.

Anyway, I hadn't found a club I could join yet. I went out to the garden to eat my lunch. There were benches and places to sit under an architectural archway. I ignored them and plopped down on the grass.

There wasn't a cloud in the sky. It was so bright outside that my eyes ached.

"It wasn't supposed to be like this."

Even after I'd learned what a unique school it was I'd entered, I was still really excited by all the possibilities there were. I've always loved large events, like festivals, and I loved them best when I got to stand at the front of the crowd and lead the celebration. How could I NOT be excited by the idea of these inter-club battles!?

If I didn't find a club to join, I wouldn't even make it to the starting line, much less get to run the race. I didn't necessarily think that I—just an average girl—deserved to be a club

representative. Even if I just stood on the sidelines and cheered my fellow club members on, that alone sounded like it would be a lot of fun.

Bimii flew over to check on me. He'd stuck by my side, without complaining, for the whole three weeks. I felt a little bad about it. Had he been right? Was I special?

Since I started school, I'd gone knocking on club doors every day after classes. So I decided to take the day off. I tried to sink down into the grass and roll back and forth to bury myself as much as possible, but then . . .

"It's been a while. How are things going? I see you're really making an effort."

It was the goddess, the granddaughter of the

headmaster and the representative of the Going Home Club. It was the model from the Mikagura pamphlet, the goddess of my dreams—Seisa Mikagura!

Whoa! It even looked like she was standing in a beam of light from the heavens. (Okay fine, she was just backlit by the sun.) She was blinding! Her very being was shining! "Why on earth would you remember me!? Am I dreaming? Bimii, go get me a drink!"

"I'm on it! Hey, wait a second! Aren't I supposed to pinch you to see if you're awake, ryui? Why would I buy you a drink, ryui?"

Damn, he got me there. I thought I could get some privacy, but he wasn't so easy to trick. He looked like an idiot, but I guess he could figure things out for himself. Right—I'd have to jot that down and make sure I didn't forget.

The most lewd thoughts imaginable ran through my mind while I savored the unexpected pleasure of being addressed by Seisa-senpai. I savored it so much it was like a piece of gum that you chew until it loses all of its flavor.

How did she know I was making an effort? Where would she have seen me? I was glad to hear her say it but embarrassed by what she must have seen. I think I was more embarrassed than happy! I quickly said a prayer, hoping that she hadn't witnessed any of the "shower thief" business. But what if she had!? Oh no! I was so nervous I couldn't speak.

Was I really this bad at talking to people? I was so infatuated with her that I had no idea what to say!

"If you still don't know what club you want to join, then I suppose you could come try out the Going Home Club. I know I turned you down before, but stop by if you feel up to it."

"Ah! Oh! Um! I'm very interested! I just got interested! I mean, I was always interested! I've been interested since the day I was born! I've been working towards this day my whole life!"

Her invitation had shocked me so much that I was babbling nonsensically.

I couldn't let this opportunity pass me by! What did the Going Home Club even do? Did they just walk home every day after class, like normal people did? It couldn't be that simple, but who cares? The only important thing was that Seisa-senpai had invited me to join! In the future, when I publish my memoirs, I'd have to dedicate at least 100 pages to this moment. I'd write what Seisa had said in huge letters on the cover. They'd probably end up making an anime about it! Then finally—finally— my homeroom teacher from middle school (single at 27 and loves to read articles about pretty witches) would have to respect me!

That last part wasn't related. I guess I got a little carried away.

"Perfect. Then I'll see you soon," she said. Then she turned to Bimii and continued, "I hope you will tell her what the club is all about. I trust that you haven't forgotten. I'm sure you know all about it."

Bimii didn't say anything. He made an awkward face as he listened to her request.

Did they know each other? From the way they acted, it sort of looked that way. She didn't speak to him politely, the way people normally spoke to instructors.

"Yes! Great! But I'd rather learn about the club from you, Seisa-senpai! I want you to teach me every . . . little . . . tiny . . . subtle thing about it!"

I raised my hand and tried to express how sincere I was. She looked a little annoyed and stepped back to get some distance. Was I sabotaging my chances!?

Actually no. She was just turning to leave. How dignified! She really must be the representative of the Going Home Club! But no—wait! I still wanted to talk to her!

I mean, come on! We hadn't really talked about anything of substance yet!

I was left alone with that unfinished feeling, because Seisa-senpai picked up her bag, turned, and left. But then, after taking a few steps, she stopped mid-stride, looking like she had forgotten something, and turned around to call over her shoulder, "I forgot to mention it, but the first battle will take place tomorrow. Unfortunately, I'm not planning on feeling very well, so I hope you will take my place in the battle."

She said it as if it was the most pedestrian, everyday, throwaway comment, but what she was saying was crazy! She didn't wait for me to answer. She just turned and continued on her way.

Who did she think she was? Could she just do whatever she wanted because she was a goddess? What was she trying to say? I didn't get it! Was it some sort of convoluted joke? That must be it! I mean, they wouldn't let someone who was just sampling a club be its representative in a battle, would they? Or was that something that she alone was permitted to do? Maybe it was, because she was related to the headmaster?

I didn't know what to make of it all, so I turned to Bimii to see what he thought. He was flapping in the air over my head.

He looked just as confused as I was. His mouth hung open and he just kept looking at me and blinking.

Besides, what did she mean by "she wasn't *planning* on feeling well?" Was that something you planned for? Did she write it down on her weekly schedule? That was like saying you were *planning* on being out of school because of death in the family.

She was already too far away to see, but I had to find some way to find the truth. The only way I could do that was to sit and wait patiently for tomorrow.

I'm sure it wall all make sense then, right? I wanted to know. I wanted to know as soon as possible! The only way to make it come faster was to go to sleep, and the only way to do that was to depend on my sleeping bag— my dear ratty sleeping bag. We'd grown pretty close over the last few weeks.

"I don't know how I'm going to get any sleep tonight."

I murmured to myself and splayed out on the grass.

Bimii didn't have anything to say, so he just nodded and chirped, "Ryui."

Movement Four: Stride After School

I went to the roof where Asuhi and I had done our stargazing. It wasn't the same time in the evening as before, but even at that it was hard to believe I was looking at the same scenery.

After class ended, Kurumi-sensei reached out and practically grabbed me by the throat to drag me up there. I don't see why she couldn't have just led the way like a normal person. Was she mad at me? Had I done something to offend her?

Oh well. There was no point in worrying about it—I decided to address the issue later. At the moment, I needed to focus on the important life-threatening situation that was unfolding.

Far across the roof from me, in the opposite corner, stood Himi-chan. She looked different than she had before. She had a serious look on her face, she carried a very large calligraphy brush, and her feet were planted wide.

I assumed that the battle scheduled for the day was

between the Calligraphy Club and the Going Home Club. What was I supposed to do? If she hit me with that huge weapon of hers, I'd be a goner for sure! Was everyone too stupid to realize that? Were they trying to get the students killed!?

"Eruna-chan, I didn't know you were in the Going Home Club! I didn't even know that Mikagura-san was looking for new members! How unexpected."

"Oh, um, well . . . I don't really know what's going on."

Himi-chan had always looked so small to me, but now she loomed much larger than she had. If she was the representative of her club, then she must have had some really impressive skills. I shouldn't have been there facing her.

Because I'd looked her up and down, she seemed to have thought I was thinking she was small, because she suddenly shouted, "I'm not as small as you think! I might look small, but I'm at least two meters tall! I can even reach the handholds on the subway! You shouldn't judge a book by its cover!"

"Last time you said you were only 180 centimeters! How did you grow so much in just a couple weeks?

What are you!?"

"I'm, you know . . . at that age."

She turned her eyes away from me. She must have been embarrassed to try and get away with such a transparent lie.

I don't see what she was so worried about. I thought little girls were the cutest.

As we were talking, I was surprised to realize that my whole body was trembling. I don't think that either Himi-chan or Bimii had noticed. All my muscles were shaking.

I wish I could say that I was trembling with excitement, but unfortunately, I knew that wasn't the case. In fact, I knew it was the exact opposite.

I was afraid. It was as simple as that.

"This is your first time participating in a battle, so I'll explain the rules, ryui. Is that alright with you, Himi-chan?"

Himi pinched her thumb and forefinger into an "okay" sign. Bimii nodded and continued.

"The rules are very simple. Today there will only be one battle, and the contestants have been determined by the academy. The stage for the battle will be the very building we are standing on. A force field has been deployed around the building to prevent either of you from leaving the battleground. When the battle begins, three life crystals will appear in the air over your heads, ryui. They will follow you throughout the battle. Although you may see them trailing behind if you move particularly fast, they will always catch up, ryui."

He'd called it "simple," but it didn't sound very simple to me. Maybe if you'd done it a few times it would be easy to understand, but as things were, I found it hard to keep my head above water.

"You lose the battle if your opponent destroys your life crystals or causes them to fall, ryui. Additionally, there is a time limit of one hour. If there is no clear victor at the end of the hour then the battle will be declared a draw, ryui."

"Heh, heh. It's rare for a battle to last a whole hour! Eruna-chan, I wouldn't count on making it through the whole hour! Better get rid of fantasies like that!" Himi-chan shouted. She must not have thought that Bimii's explanation was good enough, assuming (correctly) that I'd realized I could just run away and wait for the time to run down. If I believed what Bimii said, then trying to get the battle declared a draw probably would be my best option.

What was I supposed to do?

I was happy to hear that the goal was to attack the life crystals and not the people themselves. I guessed that it was probably legal to attack the opponent in an attempt to make their life crystals fall, but I had a hard time imagining that Himi-chan would do that to me, considering that it was my very first battle.

"How tough are the crystals? I don't have any weapons or tools or *anything!* Is there still a way for me to break them?"

"Well, well! Sounds like you're really planning on fighting to the end! The crystals aren't so fragile that they will break just from touching something, but if you got one in your hand and squeezed it, you'd be able to break one. It should be easy enough, even for girls like us!"

I wasn't so crazy as to think I had a real shot at beating Himi-chan, but there must have been some reason that Seisa-senpai asked me to battle in her place, right?

At the very least, I wasn't going to make it an easy win for Himi-chan.

As if she'd heard all my thoughts, Himi-chan smiled and stepped forward.

I raised my hand and shouted, "This won't be as easy as you think, Himi-chan!"

Slap! Our palms met in a high five.

We understood each other perfectly. Time to fight!

There weren't any other students in the building. Anyone that wasn't directly related to the battle wasn't allowed to enter the area where it was taking place.

However, the academy had set things up so that all the students could watch the battles unfold in real time by a video feed that was streamed to their devices. It was all very high-tech.

Come to think of it, that must have been why the whole building was fitted with cameras. When I first saw them, I'd thought they were security cameras. I'd thought it was weird, but then again, Mikagura is a weird place. Now I realized they were really installed so that everyone could watch the battles.

By the way, you needed points to watch the battles, too, so I hadn't ever seen one. I barely had enough points to eat, so I didn't want to waste what I had.

There I go again, getting distracted. Snap to it, Eruna!

I turned to one of the cameras and stuck a pose, then waved to my invisible audience.

Shigure and Katai-chan must have been watching from somewhere. As for the rest of the students, who knew? I hadn't really made any close friends yet. I wondered if Seisa-senpai was watching. I hadn't seen her since our talk. She must have really clung to a policy of noninterference. Still, the battle system was important to the academy—she must have been watching.

"Eruna, it's almost time to begin, ryui. You can begin the battle from anywhere in the building, so if you'd like to move, now is the time, ryui. I'll be acting as the referee for the battle, so I won't be sticking with you, ryui."

"Hee-hee! Don't forget that I can move, too! If you were hoping to start the battle with a lot of distance between us, think again!"

My device beeped, indicating that the battle would begin in 30 seconds. The best I could do was to get some distance and observe how things went. Himi-chan was saying that she wasn't going to let me do that. But . . .

"What? So soon? Hey!!"

Without any warning at all, I took off sprinting as fast as I could. Within a second, I was out of Himi-chan's field of vision. I leapt from the roof and swung myself on a railing into the stairwell. I ran down them so quickly I couldn't count how many steps I was skipping. Then I jumped down a whole flight.

I was running as fast as I could, but the life crystals followed me dutifully. They didn't seem to have any trouble keeping up.

I could tell that Himi-chan was running after me, but I was pulling ahead. I've said it before and I'll say it again, I'm great at sports—and not only because I've always played them. I HAVE always played them, but I also had a gift for it, an intuition on my feet. Even Shigure used to tell me that.

We hadn't started fighting yet. We were really just playing an intense game of tag, but I was getting so scared and anxious that I could hardly contain myself. I clenched my fists to keep my hands from shaking while I sprinted away from Himi-chan.

"Argh! What the hell is going on!?" I yelled, jumping down another flight of stairs.

I landed with a heavy *bang*! A jolt of pain shot through my legs, but it wasn't enough to stop me.

I felt like I was even better on my feet than I had been when I first came to the school. At first, I thought that maybe it was just because I had grown a little, but now that I was running for my life I could tell that it was something else. I was really performing well.

I remembered something that Kurumi-sensei had said. The students at Mikagura weren't born with their abilities. They awakened to them during their time at the academy. I wonder if the same thing could be happening with my athleticism.

"I was hoping for something a little more . . . dramatic!" I clipped. But I wasn't in any position to complain. There was no way that I was going to beat Himi-chan in a one-on-one battle, so I had to think of some way to use my athletic skills to break her crystals first. Think, Eruna! *Think!*

Thinking wasn't my strong suit. It made me feel feverish. But I didn't have a choice. If I just kept running and giving into my fear, I didn't stand a chance.

An attack from the front seemed unlikely to succeed. She had a giant weapon and I had nothing. I'd never get close enough. And of course, she was more experienced in battle than I was. So that wasn't going to work. Trying to find another route, I desperately looked for another option.

"Found it!"

A small space immediately jumped out at me. I maneuvered myself inside of it. No use sitting around and overthinking things! I'd have to settle the battle with one attack. That was the only chance I would get.

Since I'd started running, I'd realized that the crystals would respond to what I was thinking and doing. I wanted them as far away from her as I could get them, so instead of having them float in front of me, I set one to the left, one to the right, and one behind me.

There was a loud noise coming from somewhere nearby. I looked all over for the source of it, but I wasn't able to find anything. Finally, I realized it was the pounding of my heart in my chest. I couldn't tell if my powers of perception had just become exceptionally sharp during the battle or if my heart was actually pounding so loudly that everyone could hear it. I wouldn't be able to find out until everything was over.

All I could do was hold my breath and wait. But I

hated sitting around in silence! I was anxious, sure, but I had never felt time crawl by so slowly in my whole life.

"Eruna-chan! Come on out! It's dinnertime!"

The linoleum hallway was silent, save for Himi-chan's sweet voice echoing off the walls.

I held my breath.

I'll explain to make sure I'm not misunderstood. She wasn't about to lure me out with an invitation like that. It's just that I'd been holding my breath to not give away my hiding place, and my mouth had filled with spit in the meantime. She knew that I hadn't had a good meal in weeks, so I guess she thought I'd come trotting out like one of Pavlov's dogs at the mere mention of food. Well I wasn't that weak . . . really! I swear!

Whew! I wiped the sweat from my forehead. I'd almost given myself away. After I settled into my hiding place, I'd realized that I was in view of one of the cameras. I didn't want the rest of the school to see me looking pathetic.

"Come on! Hey! What are all these girls doing walking around in their bathing suits? What an opportunity!"

She wasn't a good liar. What did she even mean by calling that an "opportunity?" Didn't she know about the Internet? I could look at girls in bathing suits all I wanted! If she thought I was that easy to trick, she had another thing coming!

I guess I had leaned out a little bit—almost automatically—but I caught myself and slipped back out of view before I could give my position away. The camera had almost caught me acting like an idiot.

Judging by the sound of her voice, Himi-chan was definitely getting closer. I looked at my device, and it said that only ten minutes had passed since the battle had started. Physically, I wasn't tired at all, but emotionally I was run ragged. When she'd said that battles never used the whole hour, I could tell that she had probably been telling the truth. I didn't see how I was going to manage to remain hidden for another 50 minutes.

Finally, I could hear more than just her voice. Her footsteps were getting very close. She must have been cautious, because it sounded like she was walking slower than a turtle and keeping her guard up, too.

She'd seen how fast I could run, so she wasn't going to take any unnecessary chances.

"I'll give you a green pepper if you come out! I don't like them very much myself."

Was she losing her mind? If she wanted to lure me out, why tell me that she was just offering me something because she didn't like them? And hey, I don't like them either! Yuck!

Whoops! I nearly started snapping comebacks at her. Was that her plan to get me to give away my hiding place? Probably not! Himi-chan wasn't that strategic. She just said whatever came into her head.

Finally, she was standing just a hair's breadth away from me. As close as she was, I'd have to be very careful not to let her hear me breathing. I held my breath and waited for her to pass by. When she went by and showed her back, I'd make my move. With any luck, I'd take her down before she got a chance to use her weapon.

There wasn't a good place to hide. I'd cocked my head to the side, thinking I needed something like a bathroom or a locker. But the place I'd ended up finding wasn't as good as anything like that. And if she came from behind, it wouldn't be enough to protect me.

I was hiding on top of a giant chandelier. If it swayed at all, the moving shadow would give me away. But I'd done a good job staying still so far.

Himi-chan walked directly beneath me. She moved cautiously and was careful to look all around her—but just liked I'd hoped, she never looked up. Good! It was time!

I ran through my plan in my head. I'd get the first one when I jumped down, and I'd get the second one when she realized the first crystal was broken and she turned around. As for the final crystal, I'd have to crush it when she moved to attack me. I'd crush it with my own hands!

It was the sort of plan that you could only use once.

If I failed, I was done for. Even if I managed to escape, I'd lose the element of surprise and be forced to attack from the front next time.

I wonder what the students watching us were thinking. Were they in the trenches with me, waiting with bated breath? Or were they laughing at my amateurish strategy?

I watched her pass underneath me, and then her back finally came into view. No need to rush, Eruna. Wait just another second . . . I opened and closed my fists. I was limber and I was ready.

Finish it with this attack. Make it smooth, and make it steady. Don't hesitate—finish it!

I jumped down from the chandelier and aimed for her crystals. I could do it!

Before I hit the ground, when I was still in free fall, I twisted in the air and reached for her crystal. I could reach it? It was nearly in my hand! I could crush it! Or so I thought.

"I was waiting for you!" Himi-chan shouted, and swung her massive brush.

I was still in the air—not good! My only advantage was my speed. I couldn't use it if my feet weren't on the ground.

Oh no! Was there no way to dodge it!?

Himi-chan's weapon was very large, so I was shocked at how quickly and deftly she was able to move it. She flipped it through the air and back again as if it were just a cheap plastic umbrella. Before I could even figure out what had happened, two of my crystals were gone.

Damn! I was the one that was taken off guard!

She wasn't just fast. She had impeccable control over the weapon, too.

The crystals cracked with a loud snap before exploding in a blinding flash of light and shattering into dust.

"How did you know!? When did you notice me!?"

I finally hit the ground and took two back-steps to get some distance between us.

She didn't look like she was ready to chase after me just yet.

"Come on! You're so fast that it was impossible to keep up! I knew you wouldn't be able to run away if I caught you in the air, so I walked around pretending not to look up! I was hoping you'd do something like that!"

She'd tried to get me to attack her from above? I had already picked my hiding place before I'd been able to see how she was looking for me. I had decided to attack from the air, because she hadn't been looking up. But I guess that she was right in a way. No matter where I hid, I wasn't going to be able to attack her from the front, back, or sides. I guess I probably would have ended up trying something similar in the end.

I hadn't taken the battle seriously enough! I bit my lip so hard I thought I might start bleeding. But I couldn't turn the clock back, and there was no use dwelling on it.

I had to run away, hide, and buy myself the time to come up with a new plan of attack for my little opponent.

Once I had some distance to work with, I turned and ran. I didn't have enough time to look back, but I could feel the wind from her brush at my back.

"You think I'm gonna let you run away again? I think we've seen enough of that! Let's just get this over with!"

Her voice was so cute! I couldn't think of anything to say in response. I couldn't even come up with a joke. If I took the time to talk, I was sure I'd end up with my last crystal broken.

I was screaming on the inside, but I kept running and focused on moving my legs.

Eventually, because I was faster than she was, I felt less pressure coming from behind. I realized that she wasn't following me anymore.

"Jeez! I didn't even break one of her crystals! This is HARD! She's way stronger than I am, so isn't this a little unfair? If this were a video game, I would have thrown it at the wall by now! If there's a God, why isn't he helping me!?"

As usual, I only thought about the existence of God

when I thought he could help me.

I had been so focused on escaping that I hadn't looked around to see where I was going. Where was I?

There was a very old-looking wall that I hadn't seen before. I'd ended up in a hallway that seemed to have never been cleaned, because the floor was covered in a blanket of dust.

I'd never had a reason to go down there, so I'd never seen the place before, but it seemed to be tunnel that led to the old school building. I was surprised that the battlegrounds included such out-of-the-way places. Why did they need to be so big?

Despite their expansive size, I still couldn't see myself avoiding Himi-chan for the remainder of the battle. All I had to do was protect my last crystal until the time ran out! I didn't doubt my own athleticism, but I couldn't realistically expect to keep up a sprinting pace for the whole time either. My legs weren't going to be able to handle that kind of abuse.

On the other hand, Himi-chan didn't seem to be tired at all. She only expended energy when it was necessary, which made it clear that she really knew what she was doing.

Anyway, she was out of sight for the moment, so I took a break to plan my next move.

I slowly made my way through the old school building, looking for a room that wouldn't attract unnecessary attention.

After walking for a short time, I came across a room that not only looked unkempt but also had a notice written on its door in a mysterious language I had never seen before. I couldn't read it, but for some reason I thought I knew what it said: "Keep out!"

Himi-chan would probably be too scared to go inside. Okay, that was probably just wishful thinking on my part, but at the very least, I bet she'd hesitate before going in.

I know that I had just prayed to God a few minutes ago, but the truth is I'm not a superstitious person at all. I wasn't afraid to enter a spooky room in an abandoned building. I hummed a little tune to myself and reached for the doorknob.

Clang!

It sounded like the lock had broken, and the knob turned easily. When I pushed the door open, the notice that had been posted over it ripped in half and fluttered to the ground.

"Ugh! It's so stuffy in here! What is this place?"

I went inside and closed the door behind me. The lock must have been broken. I decided not to worry about it and looked around the room. It was much smaller than I expected—more like a walk-in closet, really.

There was a small window on the far wall and a weak ray of light shone through it to illuminate the interior, which was completely buried under a thick layer of dust. A small altar was affixed to the wall.

"What is this place? It looks like a good place to hide."

If she found me in there, I'd have no way to escape. If she found me, it would be the end of the battle for sure. But then again, I don't think a normal person would want to enter a room like that.

The strange writing on the door and now a mysterious altar . . . Something was strange about the place. That much was certain. I couldn't shake the feeling that something terrible had happened there in the past. My friends had given me a thin book once (it was a manga about cute boys falling in love with each other) and I'd learned from it that this kind of thing was an "invitation" of sorts. It was a little sad that I could remember everything I read in manga but nothing from my actual classes.

I took a breath and shook the tension out of my shoulders. There was nothing to be scared of. I reached out and touched the altar.

The moment I touched it, everything went dark and I fell unconscious.

I wasn't particularly tired, and I hadn't fainted. I was just suddenly in a different place.

I was surrounded by a pale light.

There was no sky above me and no ground below me—just a steady, bright light that surrounded and filled the empty space.

I was conscious again, but I couldn't move my body. I tried to speak, but I couldn't do that either. I couldn't even close my eyes.

Suddenly, there was a mysterious young girl standing before me. I thought that I had seen her somewhere before.

Maybe she just looked like someone I knew, but I couldn't quite put my finger on who it was.

The light was too bright to see her clearly.

She just stood there, looking up at me and smiling.

My mind ran in circles trying to figure it all out. I felt like I was in a dream. I was very happy, happier than I'd ever been, and I felt a sincere nostalgia for . . . something.

The girl opened her mouth and began to speak. Her voice was wispy and light.

"You are a descendant of the chosen bloodline. You alone have the ability to change the academy."

I could hear her very clearly, as if she was stimulating my eardrums directly. I couldn't make much sense of what she was saying. She didn't wait for me to respond but continued speaking softly.

"You must awaken. It has always been within you."

The moment she finished her sentence, the very core of my being was filled with a burning heat. The heat swelled and grew until it filled my whole body, all the way to the tips of my toes. It felt almost . . . familiar.

A second later I was back in the room. The light faded away and the last thing I saw was the girl's face. She looked like she was pleading for something.

Back in the room my head felt heavy and slow, as if I

had just woken up. Very little time had passed. I felt like I had met someone, but my memory was so fuzzy that I couldn't really remember what had happened.

"Was it my old homeroom teacher (single at 27 and stalks her ex-boyfriend on Facebook)?"

That wasn't it! Of course not! It was someone . . . younger. She hadn't been trying to hide her real age under makeup. If anyone heard me talking like that, my life would be in danger!

I felt like a flame had been lit somewhere deep within my body.

It was like I'd gained something or, no—remembered something.

I looked down at my palms in amazement and confusion. What had just happened? My head was full of noise and fuzz. I knew the answer was in there, but I couldn't get to it.

I stepped out of the small room and stretched.

Then I saw Himi-chan. She was standing there in the dusty hallway.

"THERE you are! I knew you were hiding somewhere around here. You're new here so you probably didn't know, but this whole area is off-limits, okay? You'll get in trouble!"

"What? Hey, wait a second! I haven't thought about how I'm going to fight you yet! Let's join forces! Why fight when we can stand together?"

I'd been planning to attack her from behind. Now that I'd lost the element of surprise, I had to find some other way out of the mess I was in.

"No way! You know we are almost out of time. I want to finish this and go get some snacks! I won't let you get away this time," she said. She smiled and readied her giant brush. The hallway was very narrow and led to a dead end. There was no way for me to escape.

Well, I'd done all that I could, but I guess what's done is done. Seisa-senpai, I'm sorry I failed you. In return, you can have me! I'll do whatever you want!

The saddest part was that I could easily picture Seisa ignoring my apologies completely.

"Alright, let's finish this. Here I come!" Himi-chan shouted, and she took off like a shot—straight for me! There was no room for me to avoid it, and I didn't have a weapon that could realistically block a powerful attack. Did I have to give up?

I knew that this would be the end of the battle, but I didn't want to just stand there and wait for defeat.

I rushed forward, hoping to at least break one of her crystals on my way down.

What would happen next, I thought, was obvious. My attack would never reach her. Himi-chan's giant brush would shoot right through my last crystal. That would be the end of it—or at least, that's what I thought.

Why is she so slow? Why can I see exactly where her attack will land?

Everything seemed to be moving in slow motion, much slower than the last attack when she had broken two of my crystals.

It was really easy to dodge her attack! I could slip under it to the left and run out of the hallway to lose her.

"What? How? You just slipped right by . . ."

Himi-chan was confused because I had slipped around behind her without any effort and without taking any damage from her attack.

I couldn't believe it myself.

I was suddenly able to move in a completely new way!

I suddenly remembered Kurumi-san talking about how abilities could awaken.

"What's happening to me? I feel so light! I can move

as fast as I can imagine! No, I can move even faster! This is so exciting!"

I discovered that my muscles had stopped trembling. The warmth that was spreading through my body completely erased any traces of fear or anxiety that I'd had.

"What just happened? You're acting like a different person! Oh no! Did you have to awaken *right now*? Oh well, I guess I have to get serious now!" Himi-chan chirped. She started to quickly fling her brush around, as if she were writing in the air.

"Hya! Lovely Ink!"

That must have been the name of the attack that she was using. The kanji she'd been tracing in the air suddenly appeared, floating there in black ink.

"You wrote 'fu' and 'kyosha?' Why the shogi* theme? You're in the Calligraphy Club!"

"Hee-hee! Oh, you'll see soon enough!"

She nodded at the floating kanji, and they suddenly sprang to life and started moving on their own. The fu tottered forward slowly, listing to the left and right, while the kyosha shot forward at an unbelievable speed. They were all aiming straight for my crystal.

"What's going on!? There's too many of them! How am I supposed to dodge all of these things!?"

I was complaining, but as the words flew at me, I was able to identify their trajectories and avoid each one. Huh? It was actually kind of easy! I batted some of them away and ducked under the others.

"This is kind of fun! I could get used to this battle thing, right, Himi-chan!?"

"What are you talking about!? Why aren't they hitting you? I guess I need to make more!"

She started spinning her brush and making more kanji in the air. I was having fun, but I wasn't going to win if I just kept avoiding her attacks. I had to find some way to get her crystals.

I ran through different possibilities in my head, but before I could think of anything my eyes instinctively shot straight to my fingertips. I didn't know why, but I held up my index finger and thumb to make the shape of a gun.

Suddenly, I felt like I could hear the mysterious girl from before whispering in my ear.

"You are a descendant of the chosen bloodline. You alone have the ability to change the academy. You must awaken. It has always been within you . . ."

I'd always had the power. It had just been asleep.

I wasn't confused anymore. I felt like I'd always known what would happen next.

My device was beeping, as if to alert me that my power had been awakened. There was something written on the screen.

"Ability: Toy Gun"

Right. That was the name of my special ability.

No one had to teach me how to use it.

I already knew what to do.

I imagined all of my energy flowing down and gathering in my fingertip.

I held out my finger, like a gun, and pointed it at Himi-chan. Then I fired.

"Tension MAX! GOOOOOOOOO!"

I shouted, and at the same time, a massive ball of light burst from my fingertip.

It didn't fly straight, but zipped around the room

destroying all of the kanji that Himi-chan had written. Then, as if it hadn't done enough damage, it turned and shot straight for Himi-chan's crystals, shattering all three at once.

Himi-chan was so shocked she had nothing to say. She just stood there with her mouth agape. She didn't even move until all her crystals were gone.

"What the . . . Eruna-chan . . . What did you do?" she whispered, unable to move—unable to do anything but watch the dust of her crystals settle and then vanish.

I didn't know what had happened any more than she did. It was like my body had moved on its own. I wanted to know what was going on just as badly as she did! Had *I* just done that? Was that really my . . . my ability?

"I . . . I won? Did I . . . Did I just beat you?"

"Wow! I didn't know that you could use your abilities without a special item! Eruna-chan, did you really have a weapon stashed away somewhere? I didn't notice!"

I didn't have any special items, at least not that I was aware of. It was just that something deep inside me awakened, and it filled my whole body with swirling heat. It felt like that *something* had moved my body for me.

A video played on the device in Shigure's hand. It showed all of Himi Yasaka's crystals breaking at once.

Shigure nodded and removed his glasses. Then he smiled and looked up at the sky.

"Eruna-chan, you've finally awakened."

Afterword

Thank you for picking up my book. Please call me Last Note.. I normally spend my time making music, but this book in your hands is my debut novel.

The truth is I've done a lot of different things, but none of them ever caused me to think about my signature. Then one day a fan asked my well-known friend for his signature, and I was there to watch the signing take place. I couldn't resist chiding him afterward.

"Famous people sure are different from the rest of us! Hey, when did you first realize you'd have to figure out your signature? Was there a moment when you thought, 'I'm getting really popular, so I better figure it out soon?" Did you try a bunch of different signatures out? How did you decide on the best one? Hey! Tell me the truth! Tell me!"

I think I was starting to annoy him, but now that my first novel has been published, I've realized that the time to think about my own signature has finally come. I've been warned that bookstores will ask me to sign their posters.

The first thing I thought was, "I better come up with something cool! I'm going to be so busy! I wonder if there will be a line for my signature?" and so on. I got so excited about coming up with a cool signature that I even forgot to write the book for a little while.

I soon realized that the more you think about it, the harder it gets to write it and the less natural the signature looks.

I started to get worried, so I searched for "Signature Design" on the Internet to see if I could find any tips. It wasn't long before I discovered something remarkable—a specialist that helps people design their signatures. The service itself was very impressive. They would come up with a number of designs for the client to choose from. There was so much freedom! I knew I'd stumbled on the best option.

Without stopping to think, I immediately abandoned the half-formed ideas I'd come up with on my own and placed an order. Then I had to wait a few days, but then the designs arrived! I picked the best one and received a sheet of paper detailing the steps to reproduce the signature.

As it turns out, signature design is a complicated process, and learning to reproduce a perfect signature is pretty challenging as well. They told me I'd have to practice according to the instructions they provided. I did practice a little, but it was harder than I'd expected.

Eventually, my editor made me practice. They stood there lording over me while I unfurled a poster and proceeded to sign it under his watchful gaze (and I had to write it five times before I got it correct). I made it through that surreal experience just fine, but when the novel went on sale and they organized events for me to attend, I didn't want to embarrass myself by getting the signature wrong in public.

I could have printed out the instructions and kept them in front of me during book signings, but that would take too much time and it wouldn't look very cool. I didn't want to confuse my prospective fans!

I made up my mind. There was only one thing to do. I'd have to practice every night before I went to bed.

I encouraged myself as I dutifully practiced, telling myself that *it's all about momentum! Signatures are all about momentum! Angling the letters here looks better!* I had to encourage myself as I worked, because it's actually very isolating to practice your signature in solitude. I was so serious about it that my friend would have been shocked to see the about-face I'd made.

But I committed myself to the task at hand. All of my efforts would pay off when I sat down at a book signing and my pen slid over the paper, leaving perfectly formed signature after perfectly formed signature.

I asked my editor about it yesterday. "Um . . . when the book goes on sale, we're going to have a book signing somewhere, right?"

"Nope! None at all! Did you want to?"

That's right—no books signings. Not even one. Not that I'm going to cry about it. I'm not crying! I swear!

The book you now hold is called *Mikagura School Suite Volume 1*, which of course implies that there will be a second volume. So here's what I'd like from you, dear reader. If I'm lucky enough to have a book signing for volume 2 and you see me sitting there studying my signature instructions in silence, please don't laugh at me!

You see, I was so disappointed that I set the signature aside, and I've half-forgotten it by now. If I don't follow the instructions to the letter, the signature comes out all wrong—warped and bloated.

Mikagura School Suite videos and songs are up on NicoNico Douga. Take a look and have a listen!

http://www.nicovideo.jp/mylist/22274906

Last Note.

Translator's Notes

Niconico Douga is a popular video sharing website in Japan with the unique feature of user comments being overlaid directly on the video itself, synced to a specific playback time.

Golden Week is a period in late April and early May, with a cluster of national Japanese holidays, which allow many workers and students a week of vacation.

Kurumi is a combination of the Japanese phonetic way to write the English word "cool" and the kanji for beauty, which can be read "mi."

Kansai is a southern central region on Japan's main island of Honshu. The dialect of the region is often characterized as being rough or harsh.

Bimii is a slight variation on the Japanese word *bimyou*, which means "subtle" or "not quite right." It's used as a negative expression to indicate when someone isn't very attractive.

Gyaruge are adult computer games for men that feature attractive female characters.

Debusa connotes the feeling of fat and ugly, due to the combination of two Japanese words: *debu* meaning fat and *busu* meaning ugly.

Chuunibyou is a modern term that refers to a period of middle school angst that young adults often go through, literally translated as "middle school second-year syndrome." It is characterized by a young adult's tendency to act superior and/or a belief that they have special powers.

Hakama are a type of traditional Japanese clothing. They cover the lower half of the body and tie at the waist.

Kappa is a legendary, fictional beast from Japanese mythology believed to live in rivers, characterized by reptilian skin, a beak, and a plate on its head.

Henna-chan uses the word *hen* meaning weird or strange and the phonetic ending in Eruna's name, *na*.

Chanko nabe is Japanese hot-pot dish well known as a sumo wrestler favorite.

NEET is an acronym that stands for "not in education, employment, or training." It was first used in the United Kingdom but has spread to other countries. It is now widely used in Japan.

Seiza, literally translated as "proper sitting," is a formal way of sitting in Japan. It consists of sitting on your heels with your legs tucked underneath you. For those not used to it, it has the tendency to put your legs to sleep.

Shogi is a two-player strategy board game similar to chess. The "fu" piece is similar to a pawn, and the "kyosha" is the lance, which moves directly forward.

Mikagura School Suite: Stride After School Vol 1

© Last Note. 2013
First published by KADOKAWA CORPORATION in 2013 in Japan.
English translation rights arranged by One Peace Books
under the license from KADOKAWA CORPORATION, Japan.

ISBN: 978-1-944937-33-1

Written by Last Note.
Character Design by Akina
English Edition Published by One Peace Books 2017

Printed in Canada

1 2 3 4 5 6 7 8 9 10

One Peace Books
43-32 22nd Street STE 204 Long Island City New York 11101
www.onepeacebooks.com